Die drei ???®

Die drei ???®

Poisoned E-Mail

von
Ben Nevis

Aus dem Deutschen ins amerikanische Englisch übertragen von Andreas Zantop

Kosmos

Umschlagillustration von Silvia Christoph, Berlin
Umschlaggestaltung von Aiga Rasch, Leinfelden-Echterdingen

ISBN 3-440-10065-0

Die deutsche Originalausgabe erschien unter dem Titel
“Die drei ??? – Gift per E-Mail” bei Franckh-Kosmos Verlags-GmbH & Co. KG.
(ISBN 978-3-440-10353-1)

Übersetzung: Andreas Zantop
Bearbeitung: Ursula Tzavaras
Redaktion: Martina Zierold
Produktion: DOPPELPUNKT Auch & Grätzbach GbR, Stuttgart
Printed in the Czech Republik / Imprimé en République tchèque

Die drei ???®

Poisoned E-Mail

Wanted: A Detective

Completely **tired out**, Peter threw his gym bag into the corner. "Phew, that swim training today was really tough. And all this just for the school championships!"

"Ah, come on!" Justus grinned. Swimming was just about the only sport in which he could keep up with Peter, sometimes even beating him – at least in the breast stroke discipline. Today again, he was faster than Peter. **Boastful**, he stretched his chest. "Here, look at this: I'm totally relaxed. I've still got power for another mile ..."

"Stop boasting!" Peter replied offended. "Fat swims on the surface, after all."

That was an **innuendo** at Justus's impressive weight, but the First Detective was much too good-humored to be annoyed by Peter. "I'll beat you at the school championships," he announced full of self-confidence and looked around. "Where is Bob? When we took the corner with our bikes he was still right behind us!" As usual, the three detectives had started sprinting the last distance towards the junkyard to find out who would be first, eventually.

Justus put aside some music magazines so that he could take a look at the phone answering machine the detectives had installed in their headquarters. The red flashlight signaled that they had received several phone calls.

Justus was particularly proud of the phone system with the self-built loudspeaker. But the old **trailer** was good for quite a few

---

tired out – erschöpft, erledigt; **boastful** – prahlerisch, sich rühmend; **innuendo** – Anspielung, versteckte Andeutung; **trailer** – Wohnwagen

more surprises inside: computer, photo lab and various materials for **investigations** added up to nearly professional detective equipment. It wasn't always the very newest stuff that they collected, because the three boys just didn't have the money for it. But at Uncle Titus's junkyard where the headquarters of die drei ??? were located there were always some **disused** pieces of equipment which the detectives swiftly repaired and set up for their own purposes. Same with the periscope with which they could observe the area surrounding the trailer. While Justus was listening to the calls that had come in Peter sat down in front of the **peephole** and kept an eye out for Bob.
The first caller who left a message on the answering system was Aunt Mathilda, Titus Jonas's wife. After the death of Justus's parents, the couple took him in as a **foster child**. Unfortunately, it was a favorite **pastime** of Mathilda to give out work orders. Respectfully, Justus listened to the message she left.
"Hi, Justus! Where are you hanging out again? You boys **were supposed to** help me in the garden today! The **soil** has to be dug up. Did you forget?"
"No," said Justus in the direction of the phone answering system. "But I have left you a note, Auntie. Swim training. You seem to have a tendency to ignore these messages …"
The next voice on the answering system was Kelly, Peter's girlfriend. She asked if he would like to go to the movies with her on Saturday night. If so, she would book some tickets in advance.

---

investigations – Ermittlungen, Untersuchungen; **disused** – ausgedient, nicht mehr genutzt; **peephole** – Guckloch; **foster child** – Pflegekind; **pastime** – Zeitvertreib, Lieblingsbeschäftigung; **to be supposed to** – etwas sollen; **soil** – Erde, Erdboden

"What will be showing?" Justus asked his friend.
Peter looked up from the periscope. He still hadn't discovered Bob. "It's going to be a long night with three movies: 'Psycho', 'The Birds', and 'Vertigo'."
"Not bad. I hope you'll be able to watch the third one as well."
"What do you mean?"
Justus grinned. For a few weeks, Kelly and Peter had stopped fighting and arranged themselves again, and promptly they were **canoodling** just about everywhere.
Another call was coming in, and the answering system started running. "For sure it's Aunt Mathilda; I guess she found the note and now she wants to tell me she's sorry," he guessed.
But then a female voice, unknown to him, sounded through the speaker.
The woman seemed a little **insecure**. "Hello … this is Meg Baker. I need help. It's about … **jellyfish**, yes, these awful creatures in the ocean; they have attacked me by e-mail! How can I describe it? Oh, I hate talking to answering machines! The jellyfish was hidden in an e-mail addressed to me … and now the poison is in my computer! It's shocking! You can't imagine this … You are detectives, aren't you? I've got your phone number from a friend of mine that you had helped out once before. I urgently have to talk to you. I expect you to call me back soon!"
She left a telephone number on the system. Then the tape stopped.
Justus looked at the display. "She called two hours ago," he said. "We shouldn't waste any time and call her back immediately."
"Call back whom?" The door suddenly opened and Bob

---

to canoodle – knutschen, schmusen; **insecure** – unsicher, verunsichert; **jellyfish** – Qualle(n) stepped in. He had caught Justus's last words. But actually it didn't really interest him. Under his left arm he carried a bike tire. His face spoke volumes. "When I turned around the corner I hit a nail. Flat. Fortunately, it's only the front tire. You guys could have waited for me, really!"

Bob looked so angry that Justus had to laugh. "We'll take care of your bike later. Looks like we've got a new case. One Mrs. Baker left a message on the answering system and said something about jellyfish poison in her computer."

The third detective stared at him as if Justus had just announced the arrival of **extraterrestrials**. "Jellyfish poison in the computer? These blubbery transparent creatures I'm always afraid of when swimming in the ocean? Seems to me, the lady has confused her computer for her aquarium."

"How funny," Justus answered. "She sounded more like she felt threatened."

"It does sound really strange," Peter remarked. "Probably a computer virus. I guess she caught it per e-mail and now it's creating **havoc** in her computer. In that case, she would need the help of a computer expert rather than ours."

"Someone like Tom." Justus picked on his lower lip. Tom was a classmate who was rather silent but otherwise quite okay. Outside of school he seemed to be busy on his computer all the time. From time to time he sent Justus strange mails that obviously were supposed to be funny. Actually he was sending more mails than he was talking.

"Didn't Tom once own an aquarium?" Bob asked.

"That's right! Back when he was still putting up with live fish.

---

extraterrestrials – Außerirdische; **havoc** – Chaos, Verwüstung

Meanwhile, he's got them all virtual in his computer. In this way, he doesn't have to feed them any longer."
"Justus," Peter **admonished** him, "you always come up with these foreign words! Instead of 'virtual' one can also say 'seeming'."
"You sound almost like those **sulky** members of the Society for the **Purification** of Language! I prefer to express myself in precise terms, after all!"
Bob thought it was about time to change subjects, before an argument would start. "Now go ahead, call back this Mrs. Baker!", he suggested, really **determined**. "Then we'll find out what this jellyfish thing is all about."
This reminded Justus that the lady had asked to call her back immediately. He picked up the receiver and dialed her number.
He didn't have to wait long. A woman answered the phone. "Yes?"
"Justus Jonas here. Who am I talking to?" Justus asked.
"Baker. Meg Baker."
"Good. I'm calling you back because you requested our help, Mrs. Baker. You said something about … jellyfish."
For a moment, the woman was silent. "That's … right. I'm being attacked by a poisonous jellyfish virus. But actually I don't need your help any longer. I've just engaged another detective. I found a flyer with his services that he had sent out by **bulk mail** in my mailbox a few minutes ago. I'm sorry, but you guys called back too late."

---

to admonish – (er)mahnen, rügen; **sulky** – angesäuert, mürrisch; **purification** – Reinigung; **determined** – entschlossen, entschieden; **bulk mail** – Massenmail

Justus was **swallowing.** "Excuse me," he began to **stutter** in surprise, "we were … we had … we've been … we are very busy young people, after all."
"Detectives have to be there when you need them," the woman explained.
"But Mrs. Baker, that's exactly what we're trying to do!" Justus replied. "After we came home we checked our phone answering system and called you back right away!" He refused to give up on the case just like that. "Forget about our colleague. We're already on our way to help you. May I ask where you live?"
"29, Barlington Road. But Mr. Perry is already on his way, too!"
"I'm sure you would **regret** later if you didn't consider us in your choice as well," Justus **enticed** her. "Just a few minutes and we'll be with you! Promised." With a quick look at his friends, Justus made sure that this was also in their interest. Peter and Bob nodded; Bob was a little more **hesitant** than Peter, as he thought of his bike in need of repair.
"Well alright," Mrs. Baker answered after a short pause. "Your **tenacity** has got me convinced. You'll get your chance. Whoever will be here first will get the job!"
"OK, **let's hit it**," Justus shouted after he banged the receiver back into the **cradle**. He stuffed his T-shirt into his pants. "Peter, we'll take your car."
"That's in the garage for repair," Peter replied.
"Well then, let's take Bob's, even if that one is slower."
"I'm sorry, my VW is parked at home …"

---

to swallow – schlucken; **to stutter** – stottern; **to regret** – bereuen, bedauern; **to entice** – (ver)locken; **hesitant** – zögerlich; **tenacity** – Hartnäckigkeit, Zähigkeit; **let's hit it** – auf geht's, nichts wie hin/weg; **cradle** – (hier) Telefongabel

"So let's take the bikes!"
Without saying a word, Bob pointed towards the flat tire.
Justus **threw a tantrum**. "Goddamnit! If we don't watch it we'll lose the case! And we can't get Uncle Titus's car, either! OK, so at least Peter and I will drive to her place!"
"No!", Bob replied. "We are a team!"
Peter also **favored** to have Bob go with them. You never knew what ideas Justus would come up with, and sometimes Bob and Peter could keep him from **pursuing** really dangerous plans.
"You'll get my bike," Peter suggested to Bob. "I'll be jogging behind you."
Justus agreed. "So let's get **outta** here!" he prompted his colleagues.

---

to throw a tantrum – einen Wutanfall bekommen; **to favor sth.** – etw. bevorzugen, befürworten; **to pursue** – (ver)folgen; **outta** – out of

In the Last Second

They were on their way, and a few minutes after taking off Peter was already angry about offering his bike to Bob. It was still very hot outside, and after the swim training he had taken a long cold shower. But now the freshness was gone. And on top of all, he felt tired. Usually he was a good long distance runner, but the training had cost a lot of energy.

Justus and Bob were already far ahead. Peter speeded up. Barlington Road, he thought to himself. Actually, I could take a **shortcut** to get there. He jumped over a fence and ran across what used to be a **pasture** but had turned into dry **wasteland**. When he squeezed himself through the **wire-mesh fence** on the other side his T-shirt got caught in some pointed **spikes**, tearing a big hole into it. But now was not the time to get annoyed over it. The Second Detective kept running through a small side street. On the corner he caught Bus 64 just in time. Three stations, and he was where he wanted to be. From here, it was only a quarter mile to Mrs. Baker's house. Peter had to think of her call again: jellyfish poison per e-mail. What was this all about?

When he could see house number 29 from where he was, he noticed a gray Ford that was about to park right in front of the small **stand-alone** house. That was probably Mr. Perry, the other detective, trying to **compete** with die drei ??? in getting

---

shortcut – Abkürzung, Schleichweg; **pasture** – Weide, Weideland; **wasteland** – Ödland; **wire-mesh fence** – Maschendrahtzaun; **spikes** – Zacken, Spitzen, Dorne; **stand-alone** – frei, allein stehend; **to compete with** – mit jmd. konkurrieren, gegen jmd. antreten

the job! Peter gave it all. Whoever arrived first would get the job! A small, **chubby** man got out of the car. With short steps he walked towards the garden gate of Mrs. Baker's house. The Second Detective turned around: no trace of Justus and Bob. Now he had to really speed it up. It was a matter of seconds. His legs were already so heavy that he couldn't exactly control the motions anymore. But Peter went even faster. The man had already crossed half the distance towards the house. With a fixed stare Peter was heading towards the garden gate. Suddenly Mr. Perry noticed the boy and immediately speeded up his steps. Now Peter arrived. But it was too late to stop: right in front of the garden gate he banged into the man with full force. There was a **dull thud**, and they both hit the ground.
Sweating, the man got back up on his feet. His shirt had slipped out of his pants. "Can't you watch out? Obviously you don't know what to do with your energy, you drunken idiot!" He **snuffled** loudly, as if he had a cold, and looked at Peter angrily.
The Second Detective also got up on his feet. He was still short of breath but had to grin about the **embarrassing** crash. "Peter Shaw. Pleased to meet you. Detective agency 'Die drei ???'. Please pardon the circumstances of our **encounter**."
Justus Jonas couldn't have said it better – usually he was the one responsible for **overblown** rhetoric.
Angry, the man stuffed his shirt back into his pants and dusted off his clothes. He had a glaring look in his eyes. "What do you

---

chubby – rundlich, pummelig; **dull thud** – dumpfer Aufschlag; **to snuffle** – schniefen, die Nase hochziehen; **embarrassing** – peinlich, blamabel; **encounter** – Begegnung, Treffen, Zusammenstoß; **overblown** – geschwollen, hochtrabend

want here? I am Dick Perry, Detective Agency Santa Monica." Peter had never heard of this detective agency before. Most probably it employed only one single person: Dick Perry himself. Suddenly he heard the braking sound of two bikes and sighed with relief: finally, support was there.
Justus and Bob parked their bikes and came closer.
"Justus Jonas of die drei ???"
"Bob Andrews. Also die drei ???"
Suspiciously, Dick Perry looked at the boys. "Die drei ???, so that's who you are. Your **reputation** has come all the way to Santa Monica. In case your showing up here is not based on **pure coincidence**, let me tell you this: this here is *my* case. Mrs. Baker has already engaged me. Ever heard of my motto? It's: *if you need assistance and you're in doubt, call Dick Perry – he'll help you out!*" He laughed sharply.
"Mrs. Baker has changed her mind," Justus replied dryly. "She decided to pass on the case to whoever would be at her place first. And if I see the situation correctly, Peter was here before you."
"You are wrong here!"
"Well, I'm standing closer to the garden gate," Peter claimed and took a step in the right direction.
Mr. Perry saw it and wanted to give a proper answer, when the entrance door opened and Mrs. Baker appeared. She was a dark-haired lady at the age of about 50, and it seemed she wanted to stop the argument amongst the detectives right from the start.
"Please come in, gentlemen," she said with a strict tone of

---

suspicious(ly) – verdächtig; **reputation** – Ruf, Ansehen;
pure coincidence – reiner Zufall

voice. "Otherwise one of my neighbors will eventually call the police! And please, lower your voice. We'll get everything sorted out over a cup of tea."
The four detectives looked at each other. Peter was the first to take the initiative and started moving.
But he didn't get very far, because a small dog that none of them had noticed until now was sitting right next to Mrs. Baker. The **pooch snarled** at Peter in a threatening way.
"That's OK, Harry," Mrs. Baker hissed, and the dog sat down **obediently**, but without taking his look off of Peter.
Peter squeezed past the dog and could feel how the woman examined his T-shirt with a critical look. Justus and Bob followed Peter right away, and finally Mr. Perry joined them.
They stepped into a house which had seen its better days long ago. Justus's eyes were immediately caught by the strange decoration: **marine creatures**, diving masks, harpoons, pictures of **coral reefs**, fish and a shark. Mrs. Baker seemed to have a particular interest in old ship wrecks. Justus discovered several pictures and drawings of sunken ships from past and modern times.
Mrs. Baker led her visitors into the living room and asked them to have a seat. Die drei ??? sat down on a sofa that seemed to come from another century, covered with a **drapery** showing a fish pattern. With a groan, Mr. Perry sunk into the chair opposite, again loudly snuffling.
Mrs. Baker heard it and looked at him with **disapproval**. Then she commanded her dog to lay down on a mat. She took a few

---

pooch – Hündchen; **to snarl** – knurren; **obediently** – folgsam, gehorsam; **marine creatures** – Meerestiere; **coral reefs** – Korallenriffe; **drapery** – Stoff, Überwurf; **disapproval** – Missbilligung, Missfallen

teacups out of the cupboard and placed them on the table. Justus kept watching the woman. Her look was fixed, but her eyes showed that she was slightly nervous. Her clothes seemed somehow sportive but completely out of fashion. It **struck** Justus that, despite the heat, she was wearing a long- sleeved shirt and long wide pants.
His thoughts wandered to another point: he realized that Peter – with his torn T-shirt and his sweaty face – didn't really make the best impression on Mrs. Baker. How were they supposed to convince the woman that, compared to Dick Perry, they were the better detectives? It wasn't easy to find the right **approach**.
"Do you live here all by yourself?". He made his first move forward, a little hesitant still.
Mrs. Baker nodded. "For ten years, yes. Tea, gentlemen?" Mrs. Baker looked round. "You do all drink tea, don't you?"
"Well yes," Bob answered. "At least the three of us."
"And you?" Mrs. Baker turned towards Dick Perry.
"I love tea," Perry replied. It was obvious that he would have preferred a cup of coffee, but it was just as obvious that he did not want to leave an unfavorable first impression.
Mrs. Baker disappeared in the kitchen.
Justus looked over their competitor. Dick Perry was a chubby man, smaller than Justus. He was dressed a little **dingy**. His detective agency couldn't be running too well, Justus thought. It seemed he was in bad need of money. The man would probably not **back down** so easily when it would come to Mrs. Bak-

---

struck, to strike so. – (hier -) jmd. auffallen; **approach** – Einstieg, Ansatz; **dingy** – schmuddelig, schäbig; **to back down** – nachgeben, einen Rückzieher machen

er's job. But Justus didn't want to back down, either. He was much too curious to do so, and besides, for him the **honor** of die drei ??? was **at stake**.
Perry could feel his look and bent forward. "This is *my* job," he hissed. "Do you guys understand? You guys are just amateur detectives. And stupid idiots on top. Let me give you some advice: search for runaway cats, flownaway parrots, kids stealing stuff. But don't **tamper with** the affairs of professionals!"
Before one of the three detectives could react, Mrs. Baker returned from the kitchen with a tray. She served the tea and sat down in the last empty chair.
Justus wanted to take the initiative before Dick Perry would. "You seem to love the ocean, Mrs. Baker. Obviously you love diving quite a bit, don't you?"
Mrs. Baker looked at him in surprise. "Well yes, that's right. But how do you know that I ...?"
Mr. Perry **pretended** a slight cough and interrupted her. "Well, that's not so hard to guess, Mrs. Baker – not even for this boy. The pictures, the marine decoration. A simple logical conclusion. It naturally follows that you enjoy diving." He pulled out a **tattered** notepad and started taking notes. Obviously it was supposed to look professional.
Justus was swallowing.
"But since last week I'm not diving anymore," Mrs. Baker added with a bitter tone of voice. "I guess I won't ever go diving again."

---

honor – Ehre; **to be at stake** – auf dem Spiel stehen; **to tamper with sth.** – an etw. herumpfuschen, sich einmischen in;
to pretend sth. – etwas vorgeben, vortäuschen; **tattered** – zerfleddert, zerschlissen

"Because of the jellyfish," Bob concluded.
Mrs. Baker's facial expression became serious. "That's right," she answered. "You're pretty **quick-witted**."
This, in turn, provoked another slight cough on the part of Mr. Perry. Obviously he didn't like to see Mrs. Baker complimenting Bob for his cleverness. "Of course it's because of the jellyfish," he added. "It's totally clear. Lady, you're not diving anymore. On the phone you talked about these jellyfish per e-mail. No question. Absolutely logical. You're not diving any longer. After all, that's why you asked me for help."
Mrs. Baker looked at him and frowned slightly. Justus grinned. This round went to die drei ???. So Mr. Perry dared to go one step further. "Mrs. Baker, I guess, you had an **incident** with some ... jellyfish while diving." That had to be the connection. He had **hit the bull's eye**. Mrs. Baker placed the teacup back on the table, her hand suddenly shaking. "Exactly," she started. Her voice had lost all self-confidence. "It happened just a few days ago. I was diving around a shipwreck near Seagull Rock; perhaps you know this little reef close to the coastline. No longer than two weeks ago an old cutter sank during a foggy night. Its name was *Cutty Sark* ... and ... well, I don't want to give away too much at once."
Die drei ??? nodded. The incident had been the talk of the town for a short period. The captain had been extremely lucky that he was able to rescue himself despite the stormy weather.
Mrs. Baker continued. "I was diving together with Betty. Betty Sutton!" She looked at Justus and then at the other three de-

---

quick-witted – geistesgegenwärtig, schnell schaltend; **incident** – Vorfall, Zwischenfall, Ereignis; **to hit the bull's eye** – ins Schwarze, den Nagel auf den Kopf treffen

tectives. "I'm so glad I've met this nice woman! You should know, so far I lived a very quiet life, and many people avoid me. Maybe I'm a little strange. Could be, after all. And I haven't been living here for very long yet. Gentlemen, you certainly cannot imagine how glad I was when it turned out that Betty and I have so many interests in common. She lives alone, too."
Mrs. Baker cleared her throat. "Ever since my husband and I got divorced my life hasn't really become easier. Of course I was glad to get away from Doggy. He was, up to his neck, involved in dirty business. I couldn't stand it any longer. It was just too much. Well, now I've got rid of him."
"So what happened when you were diving?" Perry tried to get her back to the actual subject.
Mrs. Baker reacted with a nod. "Oh yes, pardon me. Let's take it one by one. So we were diving. And suddenly Betty was gone. I thought she had dived down into the wreck and wanted to follow her."
Now Mr. Perry thought his chance had come. "Then the jellyfish attacked you!" he interrupted her.
"But Mr. Perry, no, you're mixing this up with science-fiction novels. Jellyfish cannot attack you. They just drift along in the water. Usually they are not dangerous."
The detective from Santa Monica didn't like that answer at all, and a **sullen** expression showed up on his face.
"Anyhow: I was diving down and approaching the wreck," Mrs. Baker went on. "The ship had a huge leak on one side, probably from crashing on the rocks. Betty must have disappeared through this hole, I thought, and kept swimming forward. Without holding a flashlight into the opening before entering,

---

sullen – missmutig, verdrießlich, mürrisch

I pulled myself through the hole and into the wreck. And there I was, already right amongst them."

Mrs. Baker had spoken the last words with a lot of effort. She was trembling. "Little jellyfish, hundreds of them," she exclaimed. "Jellyfish with an extremely strong **nettle poison**. They were everywhere. I got completely caught up with them and started to panic!" With a sudden motion she pulled up one of her sleeves. "Look at this!"

Die drei ??? stared at her arm, all covered with **weals**, and sat back, slightly shocked.

Mrs. Baker bent forward and lifted one leg of her pants. "And this one!" The skin on her leg was **inflamed** and bright red. The jellyfish nettle hairs had caused a huge red inflammation on her leg in the shape of a net.

---

nettle poison – Nesselgift; **weals** – Striemen, Schwielen; **inflamed** – entzündet

Poisoned E-Mail

Mrs. Baker pulled the sleeve and the leg of her pants back down. "That will stay for quite a while," she moaned. "The jellyfish nettle hairs had stuck to my skin here all over and burned me with their horrible nettle poison. I hadn't worn a diving suit which would have protected me. The ocean out there is not very deep and quite warm."
The three detectives kept silent, and Mr. Perry also preferred not to comment Mrs. Baker's remarks. Mrs. Baker continued. "The worst is still to come! The poison caused me to react with an allergic shock. I wasn't able to help myself anymore. I wasn't able to move. Unconscious and helpless, I was stuck in this black hole. If she wouldn't have been there I would have ..."
She didn't finish the sentence.
Justus took over. "Your friend Betty has saved your life?"
Mrs. Baker nodded.
"So it turned out she wasn't inside the ship, after all, but only out of sight for some time?"
"Yes, Justus, you said it. She found me and brought me safely **ashore**. There I received medical treatment. The local newspaper even published a small article on it."
Justus leaned back, satisfied. He had showed Mrs. Baker how good he was at following her **train of thought**. Perhaps this might turn out as an advantage when Mrs. Baker had to give one party the case. The First Detective couldn't help sending a smile in the direction of Dick Perry.
Perry looked back, angry.

---

ashore – an Land; **train of thought** – Gedankengang, Gedankenfluss

Mrs. Baker took a deep breath and continued, but suddenly Mr. Perry bent forward. "Mrs. Baker, I do understand now: after all those terrible things that happened, you prefer to never ever go diving again. Such a life-threatening situation leaves its marks, of course!"
Mrs. Baker turned around to him and nodded, but before she was able to explain the situation in detail Justus added: "But psychological treatment could help you for sure!"
Mrs. Baker turned back her head and opened her mouth, but before she was able to say something Mr. Perry called out: "But it's more than just your fear! Every contact with these kind of jellyfish could **trigger** another allergic shock reaction and endanger your life! Isn't that the case?"
Mrs. Baker was swallowing and nodding. She had completely sunk back into herself.
Justus looked at Mr. Perry. Perry was right with his **assumption**. But the First Detective would have liked to come up with this conclusion himself.
Mrs. Baker reached for her teacup and sipped on it. "I'm getting all confused with so many detectives around me," she said.
"I also think one detective is enough," Dick Perry took his chance. "Pick me, the **pro**! And kick out these **greenhorns**!"
But Mrs. Baker obviously wanted to test the detectives herself. "Well all right, perhaps; but first of all I would like to know from everyone of you: how do you want to approach the case?"
As Mr. Perry was hesitating, Justus got up to speak. "On the

---

to trigger sth. – etw. auslösen; **assumption, to assume** – Annahme, Vermutung, annehmen, vermuten; **pro** – professional; **greenhorns** – Grünschnäbel

phone you said something about a dangerous e-mail. I assume you want to find out who's behind this."

The lady nodded.

"First of all, we'll take a look at your computer," Justus suggested.

"Oh yeah? Are you boys computer experts?" Perry interrupted him at once. He seemed to have his doubts with it and turned towards Mrs. Baker. "**Fake** e-mails, dangerous computer viruses – those are serious things one shouldn't mess around with! You see, I'm an expert. I've already dealt with quite a few computer crimes."

Mrs. Baker looked up with interest. "Oh yeah? What cases were that?"

"Well," Perry took a deep breath, "of course I can't tell you about it in detail ... they are **confidential**, you know." He swallowed, then his facial expression changed, and he added with self-confidence: "After all, you wouldn't want me to tell others about *your personal* case, would you?"

This seemed to make sense for Mrs. Baker. "And you?" she asked the three boys. "Are you also ... experts?"

Bob and Peter looked at each other, sort of helpless. Of course they weren't. But Justus kept his control. "We're working closely together with Tom Wood," he explained. "He's one of our classmates, an absolute computer expert."

"A classmate ..." Shrugging his shoulders with **contempt**, Dick Perry turned away from Justus.

Justus tried to ignore Perry's comment. "Do you have any idea who could have sent you that e-mail?" he kept on asking.

---

fake – Fälschung, Attrappe; **confidential** – vertraulich, geheim; **contempt** – Verachtung

Mrs. Baker's voice turned **feeble**: "Of course the mail contained the name of a sender. But I personally believe that was only a **camouflage**. I think someone totally different is behind this. And actually I do have an idea who it could be. But gentlemen, please: as long as I haven't made up my mind whom I will hand over the case, I won't go into details about my **suspicion**. Otherwise, the **gossip** will spread like wildfire, and then they'll say that the crazy Mrs. Baker has dreamed this all up."

"Actually, why don't you call the police?" Peter asked. He ignored the idea, they or Mr. Perry would go public with her personal information.

"I believe the police has other things to do than to trace evil e-mails back to their sender." Mrs. Baker shook her head. "They would just laugh at me. No, no police."

Dick Perry nodded **sympathetically** and was quick to ask: "So what was the name of the sender of this e-mail?"

"Bert's Bar. I thought to myself, what in the world do they want from you, and opened the **attachment** – but all that was attached was their menu card."

"The beach café is supposed to be behind this?" Bob asked **in disbelief**. "But why?"

"That's what's so strange about it," Mrs. Baker agreed. "I don't know anybody in that place. As I said, I believe it was just a camouflage. But I'm not an expert. This is your job, gentlemen. Find this … jellyfish."

"Well, then let's take a closer look at your computer," Justus was

---

feeble – dünn, schwach; **camouflage** – Tarnung, Täuschung; **suspicion** – Verdacht; **gossip** – Gerüchte, Klatsch, Tratsch; **sympathetically** – mitfühlend, verständnisvoll; **attachment** – Anhang; **in disbelief** – ungläubig, zweifelnd

urging Mrs. Baker. He looked around searching for it. "Where is it?"
Mrs. Baker pointed with her finger towards the room next door. "Over there ... The password is *Harry*. But please excuse me that I won't join you. The look of this **ghastly** poison is just too much for me."
Die drei ??? nodded and got up. Dick Perry followed them, and together they entered the room next door. It was Meg Baker's study and workroom. Justus looked around and saw very tidy file cabinets and a spotless desk. Mrs. Baker had a fine sense of order.
On top of the computer table next to the window they found the said object. Using his elbows in an unfair way, Mr. Perry wanted to push the detectives aside, but Bob and Peter blocked him. In this way, Justus could sit down in front of the monitor. The other three detectives placed themselves right behind him while Mrs. Baker remained seated in her living room chair.
"Well, let's take a look now," Justus said and turned on the computer. He wasn't really afraid of jellyfish, at least not of the virtual kind. Still he **flinched** when the desktop appeared: a close-up shot of a jellyfish in shimmering white.
"Is this the desktop background you had all along?" Justus asked Mrs. Baker over in the living room. "That looks like jellyfish."
"No. Everything started the moment I opened that e-mail."
"That's what I thought. Even the cursor has this jellyfish shape," Justus remarked.
"The cursor? What does that mean?" Mrs. Baker asked **startled**.

---

to urge – drängen; **ghastly** – grauenhaft, entsetzlich; **to flinch** – (zusammen)zucken; **startled** – erschrocken

"By opening the e-mail your computer got infected with a virus. Obviously this virus spreads very fast across all existing programs. I believe the whole computer is **infested**."
"Oh please, no! What's up with my files?"
Justus could hear Mrs. Baker pushing back the chair and getting up. But it was already too late. He had already clicked on the button opening the e-mail program. The precise moment Mrs. Baker arrived in the workroom, pushing herself between Bob and Dick Perry towards Justus, the screen divided itself, and masses of jellyfish poured out of a black hole. The sound coming from the speakers made their hair stand on end. Suddenly the whole screen was a **teeming** mass of small, slimy creatures.
Mrs. Baker was **gasping for air**. With both hands she **grabbed** her throat and gave a **suffocated** sound. Then she **fainted** and sank to the floor.
Fortunately, Bob could catch her just in time; otherwise the lady would have hit her head hard on the shelf next to her.
"It really made her pass out. We'll lay her down on the sofa," Peter quickly suggested. He took the woman's legs while Bob grabbed her under her armpits. Mrs. Baker wasn't really a lightweight.
As if that wasn't enough, Mrs. Baker's dog had slipped into the working room and jumped up at Peter, snarling and showing its teeth. With a well-aimed kick, Peter could **keep** the dog **at bay**.

---

infested – verseucht, befallen; **teeming** – wimmelnd; **to gasp for air** – keuchen, nach Luft schnappen; **to grab** – greifen; **suffocated** – erstickt; **to faint** – ohnmächtig werden, das Bewusstsein verlieren; **to keep so. at bay** – sich jmd. vom Leib, vom Halse halten

Suspicious, Dick Perry followed the strange group into the living room.
Nobody noticed that Justus had remained seated calmly at the computer all this time.
Cautiously, Bob and Peter laid Mrs. Baker onto the sofa. Then Bob jumped into the kitchen to bring some fresh cool water. He looked through three cupboards until he found a bowl that was large enough.
Meanwhile, Peter was looking for the phone. Finally, he found it in the bedroom. Just as he wanted to dial the number of the **emergency unit** he heard voices from the living room. He went back there to find out what was going on.
Mrs. Baker had **regained** her **consciousness**. Her dog sat next to her on the sofa and licked her face with **devotion**. Next to the sofa Dick Perry kneeled and held Mrs. Baker's hand. "Hello, Mrs. Baker, hello," he whispered. "Wonderful! I'm so glad you're with us again!"
"Thank you," she said with a feeble voice. "Mr. Perry, you have rescued me."
"Don't mention it, that's part of my job, too."
"What in the world happened?"
"You saw those jellyfish and fainted out. And then I took you and carefully laid you down here on the sofa. You're lucky to have a man with experience in your home, not just three young kids."
Peter thought he couldn't believe his ears. That was just about the most **impertinent** lie he had heard in a long time. He

---

cautious(ly) – vorsichtig, achtsam, umsichtig; **emergency unit** – Notdienst; **to regain one's consciousness** – zu sich kommen; **devotion** – Hingabe, Ergebenheit; **impertinent** – unverschämt, unverfroren

cleared his throat for all to hear. "*We* have rescued you, Mrs. Baker," he said with an aggressive tone of voice.
Mrs. Baker waved it aside. "Please don't get into another **argument**. Main thing is, I'm still alive."
Peter remained silent, but shook his head. Bob came back from the kitchen and Perry took the bowl of water out of his hands. Bob looked surprised when he saw Perry drizzle a few drops of water across Mrs. Baker's forehead. "Is that good, Mrs. Baker?"
The woman started to breathe heavily. "Thank you, it's OK," she said and got herself up. "Very nice of you, Mr. Perry. Is the computer turned off now, after all?"
Dick Perry turned around.
It was not until now that he realized that Justus was still in the workroom.
"I'm just about to turn off the computer, Mrs. Baker", the First Detective answered, having overheard the conversation next door. "It just takes a while until it shuts down completely!"
Soon after, he returned to the living room. His face showed that he seemed to be **contented** in a strange way.
Slightly impatient, Mrs. Baker asked her visitors to come into the living room again: "Now you have all seen it! Somebody is out to **harm** me! The shock had almost killed me. That's a poison assault per e-mail! Go find the criminal!" She moaned and reached for her dog that had started drinking the water from the bowl, wetting the sofa all over. "What are you waiting for?"
The four detectives looked at each other.
"Oh yes, I forgot – I have to make up my mind whom I'm going to hand over the case now. Well, Mr. Perry, what **fee** are you expecting for your services?"

---

argument – Streit, Auseinandersetzung; **contented** – zufrieden;
to harm – schaden; **fee** – Gebühr

Dick Perry felt uncomfortable about having to come up with an answer to this question first. Finally, he mentioned an amount which was an average fee for the job.
Mrs. Baker turned around to Justus.
This was what the boss of die drei ??? had been waiting for all along. "We don't charge a fee, Mrs. Baker," he explained smiling. "Your **satisfaction** is our fee."
"Are you boys out of your minds?" Dick Perry shouted. "No fee? You guys are ruining the prices! What am I supposed to make a living from? I … I have to pay the rent for my office, my expenses … and if this goes on like that I'll have to sell my little boat – the only fun in life I'm still able to enjoy!" He took a deep breath. "Mrs. Baker, a detective who doesn't cost you anything isn't worth anything, either!"
Mrs. Baker flinched and reached for her teacup. She appeared deeply moved. "Well, gentlemen … I'm ... going to make up my mind now."
Dick Perry pretended a fake smile. "Yes?"
Mrs. Baker took another sip from her teacup. "I want to give the job to a **reliable** and respectable person," she said slowly, taking a second sip. "Reliable, respectable and experienced with computers. Money doesn't matter so much for me." She looked at Dick Perry whose smile immediately broadened. "You were very nice in helping me out of my bad situation. And I do hope you are as experienced with computers as you say. Find out who this mean jellyfish is. Dick Perry, the case is yours!"

---

satisfaction – Zufriedenheit, Befriedigung; **reliable** – verlässlich, zuverlässig

Jellyfish for Tom

One could see the disappointment in the faces of die drei ???. The boys slowly walked through the front gate of the junkyard. Justus and Bob parked the bikes they hadn't used on the way back, as they wanted to walk back with Peter to **sing the blues together**. The last thing they wanted now was Aunt Mathilda to come out and have another work order ready, keeping them from getting into a heavy argument over who was responsible for their failure this afternoon. The front door to her house just opened, and trouble seemed to be just around the corner.
But surprisingly, Mathilda was in good spirits. "Well, what's the matter with you detectives? A little **grouchy**?" she asked cheerfully. "Come on in. I was at the supermarket and bought a big pack of ice cream. We have to get rid of it before it gets old!"
The boys didn't need a second **invitation**. A few minutes later they sat at the kitchen table and scooped loads of best vanilla ice cream from the plate. A small comfort, after all.
After the first load of ice cream was all eaten up Justus asked his aunt if she knew a woman called Meg Baker. "Perhaps from one of your coffee parties."
"Coffee parties!" Mathilda Jonas was **outraged** and her face showed it. "Those are well organised meetings to discuss **current affairs**! Last time we talked about a new bus line for a better connection to …"
"Mathilda," Justus interrupted her calmly. "Meg Baker."

---

to sing the blues together – Trübsal blasen; **grouchy** – griesgrämig;
invitation – Einladung; **outraged** – entrüstet, empört;
current affairs – Zeitgeschehen

"Meg Baker, yes. Of course we talked about her once before. She's only rarely seen in Rocky Beach. She's a little strange, indeed. It's probably because she lives all by herself. After the divorce from her husband she moved to Rocky Beach. That wasn't so long ago, wait a second ..."

"Who was her husband?" Justus interrupted her.

"I can't tell you," Aunt Mathilda answered and laughed. "Listen, I'm not an information office. No, all that I know is that she's supposed to have a lot of money she **inherited** from her parents who were busy in the movie industry. But she doesn't spend it, nor does she show it. The house in which she lives looks rather plain from outside."

"Right. We know it," replied Justus.

"You know it? So instead of working in the garden you visited Mrs. Baker!" Aunt Mathilda shook her head. "Probably a new case for the detectives? Well, if that's more fun for you boys ... The garden is done already. If you don't help then I'll do the work myself! Works better this way, anyway. Garden work keeps me balanced and in good spirits." She was laughing. "I believe it would have been good for you boys, too. The lady is probably a little difficult?"

Bob mumbled hard to understand, but something that his aunt had said **struck** Justus. 'Then I'll do the work myself,' she had said.

When his aunt disappeared into the living room Justus pushed aside the bowl with ice cream. "Peter and Bob, listen up! We're going to solve Mrs. Baker's case anyway! Even against her wish! And we'll show her that we are the better detectives. We'll beat this slimy Perry any time!"

---

inherited – geerbt; **struck, to strike** – aufhorchen lassen, auffallen

Peter looked at him doubtfully. "Nice idea, but I don't think this Perry is as stupid as you think." He remembered the scene when Perry pretended to have rescued Mrs. Baker, **outsmarting** die drei ???.
"And besides, we have no information at all," Bob added. "Where shall we start? We can't get a hold of Mrs. Baker's computer anymore."
"We don't have to, either." Justus was triumphant. "When you had left me alone in the workroom I was able to get everything done. It was easy to …" But suddenly Justus began to stutter. Obviously he started to realize that what he had done over at Mrs. Baker's wasn't legal.
"What did you do?" Peter asked and looked up.
A little shy, Justus continued: "Please, don't say anything. I know that we are usually not supposed to **intrude** other people's privacy. I should have asked Mrs. Baker for permission, I admit. But in a way … she had asked us for help, after all."
"Come on, what is it, Just?"
"I sent that jellyfish e-mail to Tom," Justus admitted. "Just to save ourselves time! Asking him if he could help us finding the true sender that Mrs. Baker called 'the jellyfish'. Because the name of the sender is for sure a **dummy address**. Of course I added a note for him to be careful not to open the attachment. Otherwise, his computer will also be infested."
Bob and Peter remained silent. They knew Justus long enough that they could guess there was more to his little **confession** than what he had told so far. It was written in his face too clearly.

---

to outsmart – reinlegen, überlisten; **to intrude** – eindringen, eingreifen in; **dummy address** – Scheinadresse; **confession** – Geständnis

"Well yes," the First Detective mumbled after a short pause, "then I browsed her hard disk for some time and found an interesting file. It's name was *Last Will.* That seemed to me … somehow … suspicious …"
Peter shook his head. "Just, you opened it just like that? That's a criminal act."
"After all, I only wanted to help her …"
"You are crazy!"
"And what did it say?" Bob asked curiously.
Justus shrugged. "No idea. Well, not quite. To be honest, I only opened the file for a short moment. Not long enough, because that was the moment you called for me from next door. Then I turned off the computer quickly."
"So?"
"To make a long story short: In this letter, Mrs. Baker asks her **notary public** to change her will. As she is living alone, her first plan was to hand her fortune down to a **charity**. Obviously it was a huge amount of money. But now Mrs. Betty Sutton is supposed to inherit half of it. The woman that saved Mrs. Baker's life when they were diving. Isn't that interesting?"
"So she could have a personal interest in Mrs. Baker's death?"
"Could be, Bob."
"When was the letter written?"
"Three days ago. Meanwhile, the will could have been changed already."
Peter and Bob nodded thoughtfully. That was more than just a starting point.
"And Tom has the file with the jellyfish now?" Peter asked. "Why didn't you also send it to our headquarters?"

---

notary public – Notar; **charity** – Wohltätigkeitsorganisation

"I wanted to, but it was too late. Sending Tom the file had absolute priority so that he can start his research. You saw this Perry guy yourself. If we want **to take him on** we have to speed it up big time. So what do you think? Shall we start **investigating**?"
Peter and Bob exchanged a look. Dick Perry had really driven them up the wall. And die drei ??? had a first **lead** which Dick Perry probably didn't know yet. The detectives agreed: "We will solve the case. We'll find this jellyfish!" Bob called out. "And we'll find him before Dick Perry does!"
And Peter added: "That fat little guy should watch out." He slowed down. "Sorry, Just, nothing against fat people."
But at this time Justus was willing to forgive just about everything. He was grinning. The friends were all for it, they were ready to start working on the case. Immediately he got up and reached for the phone. He wanted to call Tom to see whether he had found out something about the file in the meantime. But Tom Wood wasn't home.
So the boys decided to get back to their headquarters to send Tom another e-mail **as a precaution**.
Then they went out to the junkyard where a nice surprise was waiting for them: Uncle Titus had repaired Bob's bike while they had been out. In addition, he offered them to check a few boxes with CDs and label each one with a suitable price – a task usually done only by the boss himself. But when it came to the newer bands Titus Jonas wasn't too good. That was something that die drei ??? had been waiting for all along, particularly Bob who owned an impressive CD collection himself. Because the

---

to take so. on – es mit jmd. aufnehmen; **to investigate** – ermitteln, untersuchen; **lead** – Spur; **as a precaution** – sicherheitshalber

award for each of the boys was a music CD – of their own choice, of course.
They kept calling Tom, but nobody picked up the phone. So after work was done they enjoyed Aunt Mathilda's delicious dinner. After that, so they hoped, Tom would certainly be at home. But Tom didn't answer the phone all evening.
"Strange," Bob thought. "We're writing an important essay in school tomorrow. And Tom would still have to do a lot of practicing. Just, you know him best. He even talks to you once in a while. What do you think is going on there?"
Justus shrugged. "My goodness, perhaps he's out there somewhere. It's not forbidden, after all. Are *you* actually preparing yourselves for that essay?"
Justus noticed how Peter quickly avoided his look and stared at the ceiling while Bob was busy looking at his thumb.
At about 10 p.m. the three boys decided **to call it a day**. Justus went back into the house while Bob and Peter took their bikes and left. Tom's flat was not really located in the direction they had to take to get home, but still they decided to take a **detour**. Perhaps he was at home, but didn't answer the phone. But there were no lights in the small house in which Tom lived with his mother. The garage was open and no car in sight.
"Gone." After ringing the doorbell and nobody opening the door, Peter got back on his bike.
"Well, we're still going to see him tomorrow morning at 8 in school," Bob said.
Suddenly Peter had a strange feeling. "Hopefully," he mumbled.

---

to call it a day – für heute Schluss, Feierabend machen;
detour – Umweg

A Case for Dick Perry

When the English teacher entered the classroom all the students were placed in their seats, full of expectation. Everybody except for Tom Wood. Mr. Barnes frowned. "Tom, of all students. More than everybody else, he is still in bad need of a good grade. Is his missing excused?"
Nobody knew anything. After five minutes, when the teacher had handed out the test, Tom still wasn't there.
Slightly nervous, die drei ??? sat on the edge of their seats. Of course, they couldn't disappear now to look for Tom. The next break wouldn't start until 9:35 a.m.
Peter's thoughts drifted away from the quite interesting subject of the test ('Creating **suspense** in a detective story with Sherlock Holmes') out to their classmate who had been sitting with them in the same classroom for years, but was hardly noticed. They had gotten used to him being there, but actually they didn't really know him.
This was not just due to the fact that he spent every free minute in front of his computer. Somehow, Tom was a **loner**. Justus was the only other student Tom had cautiously come into contact with.
Peter stared at his half-done test sheet. Perhaps there was no reason to worry, perhaps it was even a crazy – but he couldn't get rid of the thought that there somehow was a connection between Justus's e-mail and Tom's disappearance. He turned around to the First Detective, sitting right behind him, but Justus didn't seem to be nervous at all. He wrote line after line on

---

suspense – Spannung; **loner** – Einzelgänger

his test sheet without interruption. Before the teacher could notice Peter's look back to Justus he turned back to his own sheet.
At 9:00 a.m., half an hour ahead of time, he was done. 'In summary, Sherlock Holmes's detective story shows the basic elements of suspense usually found in detective stories,' was the **conclusion** Peter had **drawn**, although he didn't have much to say in his test **prior** to this.
Peter raised his hand and Mr. Barnes came up to his seat.
"Can I take a break?" Peter whispered.
Looking at the other students, Mr. Barnes mumbled: "If you're all done, yes."
Peter turned in his essay, quickly looked at Justus and Bob and left the classroom. He didn't have to wait more than three minutes until his friends had left the classroom, too.
"I was far from being done," the First Detective protested, just pro forma. But he also knew that they urgently had to go look for Tom.
They took their bikes and **stepped on it**. A few minutes later they turned into the street where Tom and his mother were living. With a **sigh of relief** Peter noticed that Mrs. Wood's car stood in front of the door now. But then he realized that the car didn't explain Tom's absence in school, quite the **contrary**: it raised even more questions. Because, quite obviously, he and his mom were not out there somewhere.
Die drei ??? locked their bikes, and Justus led the way. Before he rang the doorbell the First Detective turned around. "The

---

to draw a conclusion – zu dem Schluss kommen/gelangen;
prior – vor, vorrangig; **to step on it** – in die Pedalen treten, Gas geben;
sigh of relief – Seufzer der Erleichterung; **the contrary** – das Gegenteil

front door is **ajar**," he pointed out puzzled. They entered the house and came into a long hallway. They could hear voices from the flat on the ground floor.
"Hey, isn't that …" Peter **gasped** in surprise.
"Dick Perry," Bob answered. "What in the world is *he* doing here?"
The door of the flat opened, but nobody stepped out into the hallway. "Wishing you success, Mr. Perry. Tom is my only child." That was the voice of Tom's mother. She sounded **desperate**.
"I will do everything I can for you," Perry answered in his typical slimy way. "Calm down, lady. You are lucky. You have the community's best detective working for you." With these words he stepped out into the hallway.
Immediately he noticed die drei ???. The first shock turned into a broad grin.
"Oh, the three greenhorns! I'm sorry, you guys showed up too late. This case is mine now as well!"
"What are you **lurking around** here?" Justus hissed.
Dick Perry, still wearing the same shirt from yesterday, changed his grin into a triumphant smile. "I wanted to check up on Tom, your friend. Whether he's actually existing and if he's really such a computer expert as you say. Mrs. Baker had some second thoughts when it came to my experience with computers." Once again he loudly breathed through his nose. "Of course those doubts have no basis at all. From my viewpoint that lady is much too critical. And I would have liked to tell her that

---

ajar – angelehnt; **to gasp** – nach Luft schnappen; **desperate** – verzweifelt; **to lurk around** – sich herumtreiben, herumschleichen; **to exaggerate** – übertreiben

you had **exaggerated** big time when it came to his experience with computers. But looking at all this machinery gathered in Tom's room, you seem to have said the truth this time! Tom is a computer freak. But ... well, everything is sorted out now." And with the words "Anyway, I don't owe you any explanation!" he took off.
Standing in the entrance door, he turned around to Mrs. Wood once more who had stepped out into the hallway, too. "I'll give you some good advice: Kick out these greenhorns right away! With me, the case is in best hands!" He bared his teeth. "Goodbye, gentlemen!"
"What do you want?" Tom's mother was asking cautiously. She wiped away a tear-drop from the corner of her eyes and came closer. "Are you in any way **involved** in Tom's disappearing?" Obviously she didn't recognize Justus who had shown up at the Wood's house only a very few times. She didn't know Bob and Peter at all.
The First Detective rose to speak and explained that they were Tom's classmates. Tom had been missing during the test in school today.
"What a surprise that someone is actually missing Tom," his mother said. Then tears showed up in her eyes again. She lost all control. "The police was here already," she cried. "Tom would never take off just like that. But the police ... The policeman said, many parents believe their kids wouldn't do anything like that. And still, every day more than a hundred kids would disappear. But most of them would return home after three days the latest. I sincerely hope he is right!"
"Are you and Tom on good terms?" Justus asked calmly.

---

to be involved – mit etwas zu tun haben

"Yes," Mrs. Wood had got her control back. "Although, I don't see him too often at the moment. I've gone back to work, so I'm away most of the time. And Tom is so **peculiar**."
"Would you tell us how everything happened?" Justus suggested. "Perhaps we should take a seat?"
Mrs. Wood nodded and led the three detectives into the kitchen.

---

peculiar – seltsam, merkwürdig

Lost without a Trace

The report of Tom's mother was short and shocking. In the evening she had visited a friend. When she left the house Tom sat in front of his computer as usual. At about 11 p.m. she returned home. The light in Tom's room was turned off. She thought he was already asleep and went to bed as well. When she got up the next morning at 6 a.m. she wanted to wake him up. But Tom was gone. The bed wasn't used.
At 6:15 a.m. she called the police who arrived at 6:30 a.m. In the meantime she had found out that a gym bag and some clothes were missing. The two policemen took notes and said, Mrs. Wood shouldn't worry too much: the boy was in a critical age, and they had to deal with **juvenile runaways** almost daily. For now, they couldn't do anything. Mrs. Woods asked them to check up on the front door, but there were no signs of any forced entry. Around 7:30 a.m. the policemen had left her house.
10 minutes later Dick Perry showed up and wanted to talk to Tom. In tears, Mrs. Wood told him that Tom had disappeared. More thoroughly than the police, the detective then investigated Tom's room. He also checked all windows and doors on the ground floor for traces, but he couldn't find anything. Finally, Mrs. Wood handed the case over to Perry. That was it.
Die drei ??? listened carefully. They had a few questions, but it was not the time yet to ask them. First of all, Justus had to explain something: "Mrs. Wood, we are also running a successful detective agency. I believe we are even doing a better job than

---

juvenile runaway – jugendlicher Ausreißer

this Mr. Perry. We are very interested in helping you find your son."
Bob handed Mrs. Wood the business card of die drei ???.

Surprised, Mrs. Wood took it. "I don't mind, go ahead," she said after having read the card. "The more people are searching for Tom, the better."
"Great. Can we start right away and take a look at Tom's room?" Justus asked.
Mrs. Wood nodded and led die drei ??? to his room on the first floor. Tom's room was right next to the staircase.
It was the room of a normal 16-year-old boy. Perhaps a little tidier than others. Unlike Justus, Tom made his bed, for example. Suspiciously, Justus looked over the bed sheet which was covered all over with the sign @. It was clear that Tom hadn't spent the night in this bed.
"Has anybody looked for fingerprints already?" Justus asked.
Mrs. Wood shook her head. "Mr. Perry took a look at the **closet**, the desk, and in particular, the computer."

---

closet – Wandschrank

"Did he discover anything interesting?"
"There was something that struck him when he checked up on the computer."
"What was that?"
"Well, he said that Tom had removed the hard disk before he took off. And he'd have to find out why."
"Tom took all files along with him?" Justus asked. If that was the case then the file he had sent Tom the day before was gone as well. And he had hoped so much to find it here.
"Take a look for yourself," Mrs. Wood asked the detectives.
"Just a minute," Justus was hesitating. "First of all – Peter, grab your schoolbag. I hope you have your fingerprint detection set with you?"
"Of course," Peter answered, "always on duty." He jumped down the stairs and returned with the equipment a few seconds later.
Justus pointed at the computer and Peter went to work.
While applying the powder with a fine brush the First Detective wanted to know from Mrs. Wood what guess Mr. Perry had made.
"He said that Tom had simply run away. But it wasn't clear to him why. Perhaps Tom had been running away from something. But there was no sign of anything, and the missing gym bag suggests that he had packed his stuff himself."
"Was the gym bag his favorite bag?" Bob asked, trying to be **casual**.
Mrs. Wood stared at him. "Of course ...," she said slowly, "yes, you're right: if he packed his things without hurry he sure would have taken another bag. He would have chosen the blue

---

casual – beiläufig

one up in the closet. That's his travel bag. He hated sports. He must have been in a great hurry! Oh, that reminds me: he had even left the front door unlocked."

Meanwhile Peter had taken all fingerprints on the computer and Justus tried to turn on the PC. As he expected, nothing happened. Without the hard disk the computer wouldn't start. Justus took a closer look at the **housing**: you could see that it had been opened and only **sloppily** put together again.

They **scrutinized** Tom's room for any other leads but couldn't find anything else. Finally, Peter asked Mrs. Wood for two objects which definitely had the fingerprints of Tom and Mr. Perry on them. "So that I can match the fingerprints at the computer. Interesting will be those that remain unidentified. Could it be that your fingerprints are also on the computer?"

"No, my computer is downstairs in the workroom."

Mrs. Wood handed Peter a ruler from Tom's schoolbag and Mr. Perry's plastic business card. "He had put it here on the table. I only touched it on the edge," she said.

Carefully, Peter placed the business card of their competitor in a small plastic bag. In doing so, he took a quick look at it:

Detective Agency Santa Monica
Your experienced detective: Dick Perry

Investigation, Surveillance, Research

With Dick Perry, your success is assured!

---

housing – Gehäuse; **sloppy** – schlampig; **to scrutinize** – genau untersuchen, prüfen; **surveillance** – Überwachung, Kontrolle

Peter felt **disgusted**: 'With Dick Perry, your success is assured!' – what a **braggart**." Still he had to admit that the client must like card. By comparison though, he thought their own card would look much better.
The three boys said goodbye to Mrs. Wood who asked the boys about their fee. "You know, actually I don't care how much you charge, even though I don't have much money," she said. "I just want to have Tom back."
Justus calmed her down. "With us you have engaged the best detectives in Rocky Beach. And free of charge, particularly for Tom's mom, anyway."
Die drei ??? returned directly to their headquarters as there was no afternoon class on this day. Peter started to analyze the fingerprints right away. Bob and Justus organised all data they had collected. The question whether Tom had actually tried to run away from something, which was Dick Perry's guess, or whether he got kidnapped, remained unanswered.
"The fact that he packed the bag he could grab firsthand could be a sign for both alternatives," Bob said. "Same with the missing hard disk."
Justus wasn't certain, either. "We don't even know whether Tom's disappearance is in any way connected to the file I had sent him. In any case, it's a **setback** that Tom has disappeared and taken the mail along with him."
"A Dick Perry will beat us big time."
"This **bootlicker** drives me up the wall," Justus was mad. "He should take care of cases in Santa Monica; what is he lurking around here in Rocky Beach!"

---

disgusted – angeekelt, angewidert, empört; **braggart** – Angeber; **setback** – Rückschlag, Dämpfer; **bootlicker** – Schleimer, Speichellecker

Bob laughed. "Perhaps there's nothing to do in Santa Monica at this time. Or he is **fed up with** having to deal with movie stars and their affairs and **infidelities**. Instead, he's making up stupid rhymes. What was that? *If you need assistance and you're in doubt, call Dick Perry – he'll help you out.* Very funny!"
"Racketeers, thieves, criminals, and sharks – the antidote: three questionmarks," Justus replied, grinning again.
Peter sat at the desk and hadn't really followed the conversation between the other two detectives. Now he turned around to his friends. But not because of Justus's remark; his reddish face signalized that he had come across something very interesting.
"Guys! Guess whose fingerprints I found on Tom's computer!"
"Dick Perry's," Justus answered. "He had examined the PC."
"That's right – to begin with," Peter answered. "Any other suggestions?"
Slightly **irritated**, Bob asked: "Hey, is this supposed to be a quiz game? Naturally, Tom's fingerprints are also on it!"
"That's the point: they're not. Zero points. Be seated."
"Impossible!" Justus exclaimed. "Hold on ... let me guess: there are no other fingerprints to be found at all!"
"Exactly, winner. Once again, you've got it right. 10 points for you. Because that means that someone must have wiped off the computer carefully before Dick Perry had a chance to examine it this morning."
"And this fact shows without any doubt that Tom was kidnapped," Justus added. "Because: why should Tom – being in a hurry – clean his PC and keyboard so carefully before running away?"

---

to be fed up with – genug haben von, es leid sein; **infidelities** – Seitensprünge; **irritated** – genervt, verärgert

"Correct! Somebody else took care of that: the unknown visitor. Probably the same visitor who took off the hard disk."
Bob was thinking aloud. "So Tom had opened the door to let the somebody in, because we already know there were no signs of forced entry. And then the man overpowered him."
"Man? What makes you so sure it was a man?" Justus replied. "We couldn't find any traces of a fight. Tom could have been threatened with a gun. But that could have been a man as well as a woman. Tom had to pack his bag, and then the person – male or female – disappeared with him."
All this showed a new side of the case.
Peter turned on the computer. "I'll scan the fingerprints into the computer so I can compare them more easily."
Quickly he typed the sequence of passwords protecting the detectives' files into the computer. When he checked the e-mail in-box he shouted with surprise. "Hey! Justus! Bob! There's a mail in the in-box! You never guess from whom! An e-mail from Tom!"

Tom's Puzzle

Surprised, Justus and Bob looked over the shoulder of the Second Detective. "So he wasn't kidnapped!" Bob sighed with relief.
"I'm afraid that's not what it means," Peter answered and pointed to the date the e-mail was sent. "He had sent that e-mail yesterday night. Our computer was already turned off. Look here: time: 9:35 p.m."
"Open it," Justus asked the Second Detective.
Peter clicked and the mail opened up. He read it aloud: "Dear Justus, it doesn't happen so often that you write me, but when you do, then it's **just about the limit**! Well, I dropped the stupid essay exercises and started hacking."
"I knew it," Justus interrupted him, "Tom went online and tried to find out who the sender of this jellyfish e-mail is!"
"I know you're the greatest, but silence now!" Bob answered.
Peter kept on reading: "It wasn't easy. Not even for a computer expert like me, if I'm allowed to say this. But the beach café is not the true sender! It is a camouflage, so to speak. The sender hacked into the little network of the beach café and had his evil mail sent automatically from there so he couldn't be identified. But you won't fool Tom Wood that easily! I found out the address of the true sender!!! I don't really know who's behind this, but, after all, you should also have something to do, Just. Here is the true e-mail address of the jellyfish."
"Wow!" Bob exclaimed. "Tom has solved the puzzle! Mrs. Baker will be impressed!"

---

just about the limit – ein dicker, absoluter Hammer

"Not to mention Dick Perry," Peter was happy. He continued reading: "But before I **reveal** the solution: What **are you up to**? Well, you can tell me in school tomorrow. After the stupid English test with this disgusting Barnes who is always watching out so **eagerly** that *nobody* is copying anybody else's work. Actually, you could do me a favor and let me copy some of your stuff, Just! For the job I've done for you now! **You scratch my back and I'll scratch yours**, okay? So here's the sender's address – but hold on, I don't want to make it too easy for you. As far as I remember, you love puzzles. Just for you, I've put the sender's name into a little mystery poem! So that you also have a nut to crack. If you can't get it solved let Peter and Bob help you. It's not too hard, after all. If you haven't solved it by tomorrow morning you'll invite me to a big lunch at MacBurger, agreed?"

It's not an elephant but he's got a big nose
*Every **fug** is known to him, nothing he can't **disclose***
In every country he exists and can easily be found,
*But if you're trying to find HIM, reach beyond your **bounds**."*

"Now what's that supposed to mean?" Bob asked, slightly confused.
Peter grinned and continued rhyming himself. "A nice little puzzle Tom had sent – but it **drives** Justus **around the bend**."

---

reveal – offenbaren, enthüllen; **to be up to sth.** – vorhaben, im Schilde führen; **eagerly** – eifrig, strebsam; **you scratch my back and I scratch yours** – eine Hand wäscht die andere; **fug** – Mief; **disclose** – aufdecken, enthüllen; **bounds** – Grenze, Rand; **to drive so. around the bend** – jmd. verrückt machen, den Verstand rauben

“Very funny, Peter!” Justus gave back. Instead of the jellyfish address he now had to deal with some strange rhymes. “We’ll solve it later,” he decided. “Sometimes puzzles are a real pain! Why in the world didn’t Tom write down, in plain words, the sender’s address? Well, continue reading, Peter.”
Peter became serious again and continued: “So have fun solving the puzzle, Just. By the way, I had started hacking into the sender’s network right away. His computer was totally open and **accessible** – at least for someone like me. I browsed his files for some time, I was a little curious. I found and copied two interesting ones. That was all I could do, because then our target person went offline again. I hope nobody noticed me. I’m sending you the files as an attachment. One of the files contains some strange pattern, the other one a photo. Have a look yourself. You wonder why I chose to copy these, of all the files existing? Well, they were named ‘gold’. I got interested immediately. Gold is cool. OK. And I am also sending you back your jellyfish file. I don’t want anything else to do with it. Who knows what other diabolic viruses it might contain.”
“Open up the two files, Bob,” Justus said. “Not the jellyfish file, of course,” he quickly added.
“Finish reading the mail first,” the third detective demanded. Tom’s e-mail didn’t contain much more text but the rest of it was a shocker. “OK, Justus, enjoy the puzzle. Oh man, someone’s knocking on the front door downstairs. Who could that be? Around this time? I have to go take a look. So now I end off, quickly sending you this mail and deleting it right away afterwards, to be on the safe side. Who knows, there might be other computer viruses in it. You can fight those yourself. Gosh

---

accessible – zugänglich

– this madman outside just doesn't stop knocking. OK, OK, I'm on my way!!! So take care, till tomorrow. – Tom."
"That's ... that's ...," Bob stuttered. Cold shivers ran up and down his back. "That's a first-class **piece of evidence**! Tom writes this e-mail to Justus, and at the same time the kidnapper is knocking on the front door!"
Peter saved Tom's mail on the hard disk and emptied the mailbox. "So Tom didn't want to run away!" he said. "And I'll tell you something: I believe he was kidnapped because he had found out about the true sender of the jellyfish e-mail! Here: Tom writes it himself: 'I hope nobody noticed me.' My guess is: his electronic visit was discovered by the jellyfish!"
"Really looks like it," Justus agreed. "Although we can't prove the connection yet. Anyhow – we're lucky Tom had sent the e-mail to me before he opened the door to let the kidnapper in. And if he has deleted the document right after sending it, then the kidnapper doesn't even know about it."
"Because otherwise we'd be really in trouble!" Peter swallowed. His voice became feeble: "Then we would also have to expect an unwanted visitor!"
At times, Peter's **anxiety** went on Justus's nerves. He moaned: "Come down from your panic! Nothing has happened, after all! Tom has deleted the mail!"
"For sure he's done that," Bob supported him. "And he's found out the true identity of the jellyfish! Tom is simply excellent! I would have never expected that!"
"But it's a pity that he **concealed** the address within a puzzle," Peter lamented.

---

piece of evidence – Beweisstück; **anxiety** – Sorge, Besorgnis;
to conceal – verbergen, verschleiern

"And a damn good one it is," even Justus had to admit.
But Bob was full of **zest** for action. "Let's get this thing solved!"
Justus read through the text slowly, trying to find a point of entry. "A long nose, what could that stand for? For its look? Is it an animal with a **trunk**? On the other hand, it says: no elephant."
"But it has a good **olfactory sense**," Bob added. "That's what it says in line two: '*Every fug is known to him, there's nothing he can't disclose*'. But why 'fug', and not 'smell'?"
"Fug is a little more **colloquial**," Peter suggested, who had calmed down again. "Perhaps that's more like it for Tom."
"Or the animal lives mostly on garbage. Like a rat, for example. Rats have a good olfactory sense. And they exist in every country." Bob became nervous. Was he close to solving the puzzle?
"If we enter the keyword 'rat' into the Internet search engine it will find hundreds of results," Justus said. "That alone won't help us."
"We're supposed to *reach beyond our bounds*, Tom writes!" Bob didn't give up. "Hm. The rats in Uncle Titus's magazine for second-hand articles. Rat traps. Those of Aunt Mathilda. Or … rats … rats' nests."
Justus made a **rejecting** gesture. "Nonsense! Stop it! We're losing too much time. First of all, let's take a look at those two files Tom had copied from the jellyfish."
He pushed Peter from the computer chair so as to get active himself. First he chose the file named 'gold one'. A photo became visible. It seemed to be a snapshot. The picture was slightly out of focus. Perhaps it was due to the strong telephoto lens

---

zest – Eifer; **trunk** – (hier -) Rüssel; **olfactory sense** – Geruchssinn; **colloquial** – umgangssprachlich; **rejecting** – ablehnend, abweisend

that had been used to take it. On the picture they could see a man; Justus guessed that he was around 50 years of age. He was just about to climb over a little wooden fence, carrying a small, shining suitcase in one hand. He was dressed in a dark jacket, jeans, and sports shoes. In the background of the photo they could see dark lines, out of focus, running crossways through the picture from above.
Die drei ??? looked at each other, puzzled: neither did they know this man, nor could they match the scene shown on the picture to any existing place they knew of.
"You think that's the jellyfish?" Bob wondered.
"We'll find out," Justus answered. He already had an idea how. But now he wanted to know what was hidden in the second file Tom had copied. Its name was 'gold two'. He double-clicked on it expectantly.
But the three boys reacted with disappointment: all they could see were dark lines, a structure looking similar to **veins** of a leaf. The lines split and branched out many times.
"Jellyfish?" Peter asked.
Justus turned the picture 90 degrees so that the main line was on top. "Strange jellyfish," he said. He picked on his lower lip. "Perhaps the drawing of a **circuit**? Something electronic?"
"A **family tree**," suggested Bob. "Only without names!"
"Not bad," Justus said and pointed to the screen: "But what is this dot at the end of this one line?"
Now Bob noticed it, too. "Perhaps it's a specific person in the family tree? For example the man on the photo?"

---

veins – Ader, Vene; **circuit** – (hier -) (elektronischer) Schaltkreis; **family tree** – Stammbaum

"For sure there is some connection – but what is it?" Justus clicked on the file to open the picture of the man once more. Again they looked at the picture thoroughly.
"We don't get any further just by staring at it," Justus finally said. "Guys, we don't have just one puzzle but three. And they're tough ones."
"We should call Inspector Cotta and tell him that Tom might have been kidnapped," Peter suggested. He was afraid that they were about to lose control over the situation.
Surprisingly, Justus agreed. "OK. But I'd prefer we keep our little **inquiry** with Tom to ourselves. After all, we cannot prove the connection between the jellyfish e-mail and his disappearance yet."
"But what are we going to do with our two puzzle files?" Peter asked.
"Very simple," Justus smiled. "The e-mail **avalanche**."
"The e-mail avalanche?"
"Well, meanwhile every child in Rocky Beach knows the telephone avalanche: each of us calls five friends, each of these five friends calls another five friends in turn, and so on. In every phone call our question will be handed down the line, adding our phone number to call us back. Kids have often watched something that could help us solving the case."
"Of course," Bob called out. "Instead of starting a telephone avalanche we'll start an e-mail avalanche! That's perfect! It even beats the telephone avalanche, because we don't have to deal with the '**Chinese whisper** effect': an e-mail message will always be passed on correctly. We simply mail the photo and the

---

inquiry – Anfrage, Nachforschung; **avalanche** – Lawine;
Chinese whisper – stille Post

drawing to five friends, asking them to pass it on to their friends in turn. Whoever knows something should report back to us."

"The only risk with this is that the jellyfish himself might be able to put his hands on it," Justus pointed out. "Same with the telephone. But we have to take that risk. We should add to our mails that the files should only be passed on to known friends and kids so that no adult gets to know about it."

"And we'll put a time limit on it," Bob said, "otherwise the mail will travel around the world for years and we'll be **drowning in answers**."

Justus nodded. "And we should suggest to limit it to the greater Los Angeles area."

Such a good plan could only cause enthusiasm with Peter. "Great idea! And what are we going to do in the meantime until the first answers come in?"

"We'll visit Betty Sutton, Mrs. Baker's friend," Justus proposed. "After all, besides the unknown man on the photo she is our hottest trace!"

---

to be drawned in answers – (Redew.) mit Antworten zugeschüttet werden

Pelagia noctiluca

First of all, Justus called Inspector Cotta. Without having to explain his suspicion, he managed to convince Cotta that Tom might have been kidnapped. Hard-won experience told Cotta that he couldn't get anything out of Justus if he wasn't willing to tell anything himself.

Still, Cotta wasn't really happy about the news: "I'm busy up to my neck with those cases of **jewelry theft** you've probably read about in the papers: burglary in **mansions** and hotels. The stuff is disappearing without a trace. But if you insist I will personally contact those colleagues working on the case 'Tom Wood', how about that?"

"Inspector, please, do a little more than that. Support your colleagues for all it is worth!"

Cotta promised to do what he could.

"Oh, one more thing, Inspector," Justus added.

"Yes?"

"It could happen that you'll run into ... well ... another detective during your investigations. Mrs. Wood talked to him about the case as well. His name is Dick Perry."

"Hold on ... Dick Perry ... the guy from Santa Monica? Oh, yes, I know him. Together with him and his female assistant Barbara Stevens, I gave evidence in court against a **con man** in an **insurance fraud** case. It's already two, three years back. Dick

---

pelagia noctiluca – Leuchtqualle; **jewelry theft** – Schmuckdiebstahl; **mansion** – Villa, Herrenhaus; **con man** – Betrüger, Hochstapler; **insurance fraud** – Versicherungsbetrug

Perry ... a strange guy, **sly** and **cunning**, a trickster. But it's a competition I wouldn't **underestimate**."
Justus was swallowing.
"Well, I'm curious who will solve the case first: Dick Perry or Justus Jonas. Or will a certain Inspector Cotta be the first one?"
Cotta laughed. "Well, what do you think?"
"I don't care," Justus replied quickly, "main thing is, to find Tom Wood as soon as possible."
With a reddish face Justus hung up. Because of the detective competition from Santa Monica he actually wanted to ask the inspector for assistance, but that turned out to be a big failure.
Peter and Bob couldn't stop grinning. But a few seconds later Justus was already on top again. After all, die drei ??? were able to present a long successful job record and didn't have to hide from anybody, not to mention Dick Perry!
Immediately the detectives went to work to find Betty Sutton. There were two Betty Suttons living in Rocky Beach. Bob noted their addresses and they started their search.
The first address turned out to be the right one. Betty wasn't home, but the neighbor told die drei ??? that Mrs. Sutton is often out diving. The age seemed to fit as well.
"If you want to return the **bathometer** you had borrowed, it would be best to contact her at 'Waterworld', the marine zoo. Because that's where she's working!"
The trick with the borrowed bathometer was Bob's idea, but suddenly Justus had another one on top. He pulled out the picture with the snapshot showing the man with the suitcase: "We'd also like to return this picture to her."

---

sly – durchtrieben, listig; **cunning** – gerissen, schlau;
to underestimate – unterschätzen; **bathometer** – Tiefenmesser

The neighbor looked at it for a short moment. "OK, but what are you showing me this for? Who is this?"
Justus was disappointed. "Well, I thought perhaps you might know the man? Isn't she together with him often?"
The neighbor took a step back. "As far as I know, this is not her friend. Hey, what is this all about? Who are you? Do you know Betty at all? You're **nosing around**, aren't you?" His mood changed from one second to the other. He looked at the boys with a fixed stare. "**Get lost** before I call the police!"
Die drei ??? didn't need a second warning. They turned around and took off full-speed with their bikes. It wasn't until they had taken the corner that they slowed down again.
"Obviously you're wrong," Bob said with disappointment. "There's no connection between Betty Sutton and the man."
But Justus disagreed: "It was just a try, after all. But that doesn't prove anything yet. Sadly, the truth is more complex than we sometimes imagine. Let's **sound out** this lady."
So they were on their way to the 'Waterworld'. The marine zoo was located on the **outskirts** of Rocky Beach, mostly attracting tourists. But compared to the large facilities in the greater Los Angeles area it offered only very few attractions; time and again, plans existed to close it down, but so far they had all been dropped.
Today it was similar: only a few cars filled the front parking lot on this hot, sunny day. A big sign pointed out the highlights of the aquarium: an octopus, several dolphins, and a shark. Die drei ??? knew that the shark was already pretty old and had no

---

nosing around, to nose around – herumschnüffeln; **get lost!** – verschwinde(t)!; **to sound out** – auf den Zahn fühlen, ausfragen; **outskirts** – Außenbezirke, Stadtrand

teeth anymore. The octopus had been the 'new highlight' of the zoo for years by now. Suddenly Peter picked on Justus's sleeve: "Look at this: *Visit our special aquarium with dangerous jellyfish!* This trip to the zoo seems to turn out more interesting than we thought!"
At the cashier's desk Justus immediately asked for Betty Sutton to avoid having to spend money for a ticket.
"She's at work. Come back at 5 p.m.," was the short answer of the cashier lady. "You want to get in, you'll have to pay!"
Slightly annoyed, the boys counted their dollars and bought three student tickets.
"We'll have to think this fee issue over," Peter complained. "We should have our clients pay at least for our expenses."
Justus stuffed his wallet back into the trouser pocket. "From time to time, we do get some financial support, after all," he said. "I believe there's still some money in our cash box."
"Then I demand a **refund**," Peter declared, and Bob joined him. "We've already been **dragged** to this 'Waterworld' place when we were in Kindergarten!"
They squeezed themselves by a family admiring the little octopus. The little son knocked on the aquarium glass with a little toy scoop.
Justus dragged Bob along who couldn't stop staring at the octopus. But before the First Detective could get outside to the dolphins he stumbled over a bucket in his way. The bucket **tilted** over and the water splashed all over the place. Justus was just about to pull a little black backpack covered with a dog

---

refund – Rückerstattung, Rückzahlung; **to drag** – ziehen, schleifen, zerren; **to tilt** – sich neigen

sticker out of the **puddle** when a woman came running: "Not so **clumsy**, guys!"
Her short hair was held in place with sticky hair gel and she was waving about hectically with some **pliers**. Behind the woman there was an aquarium lit from within, with two lonesome jellyfish drifting along in the water circulating within it.
The woman stemmed her arms into her hips and looked up to the three detectives who were about a foot taller than her. "Lucky you that my backpack is waterproof!"
Justus ignored the remark and stepped closer to the aquarium. "Oh, those are Forskalia edwardsi!" he said. "Really beautiful **specimens**."
The woman laughed loudly. "Wise guy, eh? But before you use zoological terms you should do your homework. This sort of jellyfish is a subspecies of Pelagia noctiluca and no Forskalia edwardsi."
"But this kind of jellyfish is dangerous, too, isn't it?"
"They can cause very strong manifestations of poisoning, if that's what you mean."
Justus tried to overcome his spontaneous antipathy towards the woman and smiled at her. "You're an expert, aren't you?"
"I'm working here," the woman answered. "Although I can imagine more worthwhile things to do than repairing aquariums all day," she added. There was no doubt for die drei ??? that this must be the woman they were looking for.
"I do believe you," Peter remarked, a little **pertly**.
The woman stared at him. "Tell me, what is it that you want?"
Justus decided **to launch** a frontal attack. "Aren't you Betty Sut-

---

puddle – Pfütze; **clumsy** – trampelig, tollpatschig; **pliers** – Rohrzange; **specimen** – Exemplar; **pertly** – vorlaut; **to launch** – starten, loslassen

ton, the friend of Meg Baker?" he asked full of self-confidence. The woman flinched.
"A few days ago you were out with Mrs. Baker, diving at a shipwreck, and …" But before he could continue Betty Sutton interrupted him harshly. "You too? What's the matter today? Just a few minutes ago this fat, sticky detective showed up, and now you three guys come around to **pester** me with questions just the same. I have more important things to do than to deal with your little problems. If you don't immediately …"
"Mrs. Sutton," Justus interrupted her, "isn't it unusual that hundreds of poisonous jellyfish gather inside an old shipwreck, just like that?"
She was gasping. "It's also very unusual to be kept from doing one's work by detectives showing up all the time."
"Why is the aquarium so empty?" Justus pointed towards the jellyfish aquarium. "Very unusual for main attraction!"
"They got stolen! And now get out of here! Come on, get lost!"
"Excuse me, but after all we have paid for getting in here," Justus dared to protest.
"Then get your money back from the cashier," Betty Sutton replied harshly. "You're not interested in the aquarium anyway!"
In a way she was right. The woman was pretty energetic, Justus had to admit. For the second time today, the three detectives had to **retreat**. But there was something more painful than the harsh tone of Betty Sutton; it was the fact that Dick Perry, once again, had been faster. Because there was no doubt who Betty referred to when she mentioned a 'fat, sticky detective'.

---

to pester – löchern, plagen, belästigen; **to retreat** – sich zurückziehen, nachgeben

“But we still have an **ace** up our sleeve,” Justus said when they were swinging themselves onto their bikes. “Remember Tom’s puzzle. Does it fit in any way to Betty Sutton?”
“She doesn’t have a long nose,” Bob mumbled. Several thoughts rushed through his head **at random**. “But that’s not what Tom meant to say, because he doesn’t know the person behind the address. What’s the connection? Is it that this lady sticks her nose in things, none of which are her business? Just, we should take a look at her flat. And look for Tom.”
“We can’t show up there right now,” Justus pointed out. “This nerving neighbor will immediately call the police when he sees us.”
“Perhaps the e-mail avalanche could help us,” Peter hoped.
They rushed back to their headquarters and turned on their computer right away. But there was only one message in response to their inquiry. Peter opened the mail and started reading:
“Hello you drey ???, I think that s a tresure map. Greatings, Casey-Charlotte. I am 7 years olt.”
“Can’t even spell words correctly but is already sitting in front of a computer,” Bob was wondering. “Casey refers to the file with those lines.”
“Treasure map does sound very mysterious,” Peter remarked, “but I’m afraid the little one has read too many pirate stories … still I’m going to send her a little ‘thank you’.”
Nervous, the detectives sat on the edges of their seats until Peter surprised them with an idea: “We could go diving for the shipwreck and take a look at it.”
Justus liked the idea. It was better then to sit around doing nothing.

---

ace – Ass, Trumpf; **at random** – wahllos

Die drei ??? knew that spot in the ocean ever since they were small children. A few years ago they had been diving near the small rock close to the coastline for remainders of sunken ships and got into an old pirate story. But once the secret of the rock was **revealed** the spot had lost its attraction, and the sinking of the small cutter had attracted the community's attention only briefly. Besides some old fishnets the boat hadn't carried any load, and it was so rusty that its breakdown had only been a question of time.

But Meg Baker and Betty Sutton had been there, and this made Justus come up with an idea: "Could it be that someone wants to keep Mrs. Baker from showing up at the wreck again? I mean: diving down to the wreck?"

Bob was about to shut down the computer and said: "That would be a new trace. You mean if Betty Sutton would not be the suspect we're looking for. Perhaps it is this man on the photo?"

"Betty could still have something to do with it. But the **inheritance** would most likely not be her motive."

"Then we would have to find something suspicious about the wreck," Bob suggested. "I'm curious whether the jellyfish will still be there."

Peter looked at his watch. "Exactly. Let's go for the wreck. That's what I said. We should be able to make it to the beach within 20 minutes. We don't need any equipment besides our diving masks. The water isn't too deep out there."

The boys had stored their diving masks at their headquarters, so they were able to head for the beach right away, climbing

---

to reveal – zeigen, enthüllen, offenbaren; **inheritance** – Erbschaft, Nachlass

down one of the many hidden paths between the rocks, leading them down to a small bay with a beach. Nobody was out here, as most of the people who wanted to enjoy the sun or the sea preferred the little sandy bays, or they were heading straight for the wide Rocky Beach shore.
But from here it was only a few feet to the rock where the shipwreck was. While Justus and Bob were still busy putting on their equipment Peter **inflated** a little plastic boat he had taken along with him. Thanks to his well-trained lungs he managed to get it filled pretty quickly.
Die drei ??? jumped into the water, turned the boat upside down, and swam out to the rock. The ocean was calm and the water clear, so it was no problem for them to arrive safely at their destination. Like a little lighthouse, the mast of the boat stood out about six feet above the water surface. Directly behind it, the little reef was rising above the waves.
With a string Peter attached the plastic boat to the mast so that the drift wouldn't take it away. Then he put on his diving mask, took a deep breath and disappeared underwater.
Justus and Bob followed him. The sunken boat rested on a slight **elevation** and was tilted towards one side. It didn't really look stably positioned. It almost seemed as if it would move back and forth in the slight underwater drift.
On the side facing the ocean ground Justus and Bob discovered the leak. Peter signalized his friends to come closer, and they did. Some fish escaped when the unusual visitors approached their territory. But before die drei ??? could reach the hole they were out of air and had to return to the surface.
They held on to the boat. Justus pushed up his diving mask.

---

to inflate – aufblasen; **elevation** – (Boden)Erhebung

"Peter, you swim directly into the wreck," he commanded.
"Never ever," Peter answered. "I hate jellyfish."
"But who of us is the best diver?"
"Well, I am, of course. But do I have to …"
"You can hold your breath for almost two minutes. We can't."
"It's a pity that you only beat me in the breast stroke discipline, Just." Peter took a deep breath and began diving. Justus and Bob followed him. They could see Peter approaching the black hole, cautiously looking inside, and disappearing within.
Right this moment the drift seemed to become stronger. Slowly the boat tilted towards the side. Bob was the first to recognize the danger: if the boat tilted over completely Peter would be trapped in it!
Alarmed, he gave Justus a sign, and together they swam towards the side of the boat. With all their strength, they pushed against it to keep an escape route open for Peter. Their feet sunk deeper into the sandy ocean ground, but they managed to keep the boat from tilting over further. But by now they were out of air. Where was Peter? Why didn't he come out?
They couldn't hold the boat up for very much longer. The urge to dive up to the surface became increasingly stronger. Suddenly Justus felt that there was something behind them. A motion, a shadow, a push through the water. Was it a shark?
With a jerk, Justus turned around. What he saw **curdled his blood**. Directly in front of him, a diver was floating, all dressed in black, and his harpoon aimed directly at the First Detective.

---

with a jerk – mit einem Ruck; **to curdle one's blood** – das Blut in den Adern erstarren lassen

The Plastic Boat Conference

Before Justus could do anything the diver was next to him. Justus had to get back up to the surface for air. He was close to fainting. Only his strong willpower helped him to stay underwater for another moment. He couldn't leave Peter alone. Bob had already dived up to the surface. With all his remaining strength Justus tried to get a hold of the diver, but the black man swam past him. The unknown diver took his harpoon and jammed it between the boat's rail and the ocean ground so that the boat couldn't **tilt** over any further. That was Peter's rescue: right that moment he slipped out and rose to the surface **in no time**. Justus followed him.
Breathing heavily, they held on to their plastic boat. The shock was written in Peter's face. "Never again," was the only thing he could say.
A few seconds later the stranger came to the surface. He took out his mouthpiece, spit out some water and pushed up his diving mask. Die drei ??? were so shocked that they almost slipped off their boat: it was Dick Perry himself.
"I should've let you drown, you **blokes**," he shouted. "First you tamper with my case, and now I even have to save one of you guys' life!"
This helped to quickly return die drei ??? to reality.
"We're just diving around here," Peter stuttered.
"Well, pure coincidence," Bob added.
"Well, we wanted to take a look at the spot Mrs. Baker had de-

---

to tilt – neigen, kippen; **in no time** – im Nu, sofort; **blokes** – Burschen, Macker, Typen

scribed," Justus said, who obviously thought that Dick Perry had not deserved such an outright lie after his rescue action. Perry didn't really care. "Next time I won't help you out! Quite the contrary! I will do everything I can to keep you from getting in my way! These are *my* cases! *My* experience is asked for, and *my* income is at stake!"
Justus didn't have any other choice than to inform Dick Perry of a fact obviously still unknown to him. "Tom's mother told us to look for Tom, too. We are working for Mrs. Wood."
Dick Perry was outraged. "She did? You **lured** her with your free-of-charge offer? Guys, this means war! I'm deadly serious!"
He put on his diving mask again, pushed the mouthpiece of the **air tank** back into his mouth, and dived down.
Die drei ??? looked at each other in surprise and were just about to break out into loud laughter over Perry's 'performance' when another shock made their hair stand on end: Perry had released his harpoon, and the arrow hit the three detectives' plastic boat. With a loud 'phewsh' the air escaped from the boat, and within seconds one half of the boat was **slack** like a supermarket plastic bag. It was only due to the second intact air chamber that the boat was still on the surface.
Bob mumbled something like "direct hit". Peter expressed himself a little more clearly: "This scumbag!", he **ranted** and dived underwater. The boat was a gift from Kelly so that they could canoe out to lonely bays together. He would have liked to show the detective a threatening gesture, but Dick Perry was nowhere to be seen anymore.
Peter came back up to the surface and swam back to his friends.

---

to lure – (an)locken, ködern; **air tank** – Sauerstoffflasche;
slack – schlaff, locker; **to rant** – schimpfen, toben

"After all, the guy saved my life when I was trapped inside the old boat," he admitted. "That's something we shouldn't forget."
"Still I'm angry that we have to swim back without the boat," Justus protested.
"Well, it's a good training for the swim championships," Peter replied and started crawling back to the shore.
When they were a little further away from the rock it became clear how Dick Perry had managed to show up so quickly: in front of the reef they saw a large motor boat swinging on the waves. Its name was *Barbara* and its **port of registry** was the Marina del Rey near Santa Monica.
The First Detective headed back for the small bay and thought over another problem. How could he keep Peter from giving up on the case? He knew his friend well enough to know that Perry's harpoon shot had made a lasting impression on Peter.
And the First Detective hadn't been wrong with his guess. They had just arrived at their headquarters and opened the door when Peter started to **hem and haw**.
Slightly exhausted from the bike tour Justus fell into the chair. He interrupted Peter so as to save time. "Listen, Second, perhaps we should indeed calm down this Perry guy a little. We'll put Mrs. Baker's case aside for now and concentrate on Tom. That is more important. We won't let Tom down, **by no means**!"
Bob agreed, because he was almost sure anyway that there was a connection between both cases, and Peter found the suggestion acceptable. In this way they might be able **to keep** Perry **at bay**.

---

port of registry – Heimathafen; **hem and haw** – herumdrucksen, herumstottern; **by no means** – auf keinen Fall, mitnichten; **to keep so. at bay** – sich jemanden vom Leibe halten

"By the way, did you discover anything interesting inside the hull?" Justus asked. In all that **commotion** he had totally lost sight of the original **objective** they had in mind.
"No jellyfish. The inside was completely empty. Obviously the ship hadn't carried a load, or they have removed it in the meantime. All I found was a chest in one corner of loading space. I was just about to swim into it when the boat started tilting over, and I quickly headed back for the hole."
Bob was disappointed. "So there's nothing that could help us any further."
"We could give it another try with air tanks," Justus said, but Peter protested loudly. "No way, guys! Did you already forget about our agreement?" Shaking his head he sat down in front of the computer and turned it on. "Let's see what the e-mail avalanche resulted in." Just a few moments later he could proudly announce: "What did I tell you? The next answers are there!"
Curiously he clicked on the mails. "A guy called Max writes, the pattern could be the leaf of a tree. Well, we had that already. The next one, Paul, had also wondered about the pattern and thinks it's a labyrinth. Not bad, that idea. The next one thinks it's a leaf, once again. Oh man, nobody has any idea about the picture. Oh, this sounds interesting. Here we have a guy called Steve Martin: 'Hello friends, I think I know just about all your adventures. You guys are the best, indeed! Say, could that pattern perhaps be a small section of a map? I don't know the man on the photo, though. Bye bye – Steve Martin.'" Peter looked up. "Colleagues, the treasure map was already one suggestion.

---

commotion – Aufregung, Tumult; **objective** – Ziel(setzung)

This one points in a similar direction. And it would explain the dot at the end of this line near the bottom."
"The only point is: what does this map actually show?" Justus asked. "What map does this pattern fit to?"
Just to give it a try, Peter opened the city map of Rocky Beach on the computer so that it was visible on the screen. Then he tried to **superimpose** the line pattern over the screen. Several times he changed **scales** and turned the lines, but no matter what they tried, they just couldn't match it. The drawing didn't fit any part of the map.
Peter gave up and returned to the e-mail in-box. There were five more messages he hadn't opened yet. "Strange, this is a message from the Organisation for the Protection of Seaweed; the text doesn't make any sense at all. Some stupids are always part of it. Uhuh, check this out: this mail from Mary-Kathy is the first one referring to the photo. Listen: 'Dear drei ???', she writes. 'I know the man on the picture. He lives in our neighborhood. Sometimes I see him when I play outside. Then he often shouts at me. His name is Jack Sharky. I hope I could help you. Mary-Kathy, 9 years old.'" Peter looked up. "Mary, you sweetheart, I could kiss you!"
Bob had written down the name right away. "That sounds really promising! Perhaps Jack Sharky might be able to lead us to Tom!"
"Check out the other three remaining mails," Justus slowed him down.
But they didn't contain anything new.

---

to superimpose – aufsetzen, überlagern, über etw. legen;
scales, scale – (hier -) Maßstab

Meanwhile Bob had taken the telephone book and was looking for Jack Sharky's address. Peter tried to do the same with the computer, but Bob won the race: "Here it is: Santa Monica, 21 Sunset Road. Guys, let's go for it."
Peter looked up from the computer. "Now right away? And what explanation should we give him for our visit?" he asked skeptically. Peter hated overhasted actions. Strange enough, he himself often got into such situations.
Justus calmed him down. "We'll just take a look at the guy," he suggested. "Perhaps we might also show the photo to him."
The First Detective folded the printed picture of Mr. Sharky together and stuffed it in the back pocket of his pants. Hastily they left their headquarters.

Die drei ??? returned with their bikes to the junkyard. The moment they turned around the corner they became aware of a gray Ford parking on the side. Suddenly the driver started the motor.
"Damn, that's Dick Perry!" Peter shouted and stepped on the brake. "He's serious!"
Bob and Justus came closer to the Second Detective. "It seems Perry doesn't believe that we leave the case alone," Justus said angrily. "He wants to know what we're up to."
"And he seems to have a **hunch** that we are better than he tries to make people believe we are," Peter was **bragging** a little.
Justus grinned. "But if Dick Perry insists on it he shall do his job undisturbed and by himself; what do you think, friends?"
Peter and Bob nodded **emphatically**.

---

hunch – Ahnung, Intuition; **to brag** – prahlen; **emphatically** – nachdrücklich

"So listen up! I have a plan: This is how we get rid of him." Justus took off and turned around the corner into a side street. Peter and Bob followed him, meanwhile listening to the First Detective's explanations. Justus's idea how they could get rid of Dick Perry was good, but it had a **hitch**. Together they kept on thinking about the plan. So once again they drove around the block. When that still wasn't enough they biked down the fairly long Witfield Road. Then they had come to an agreement. Die drei ??? looked around cautiously. Dick Perry was still following up on them, keeping a good assistance between him and them, though. Slowly he started getting into trouble with the other drivers behind him who couldn't understand what the slowdown was about.
The three detectives wanted Perry to feel certain that they were not aware of his presence. That's why the three friends still kept sticking together, biking down Main Street. When they arrived downtown they exchanged a last look. Then they broke up. Everything went very fast: Bob and Peter went straight ahead, while Justus made an abrupt right-hand turn and immediately speeded up.
Dick Perry had to make a decision.

---

hitch – (hier -) Haken

Fooled!

Dick Perry's car was **lurching** for a moment, then he took a right-hand turn as well. The detective from Santa Monica went for Justus! Bob and Peter had said that from the beginning. To Dick Perry, Justus Jonas was the detectives' leader. If there was anything to find out, then by sticking to him. So of all three detectives, the first one had to **bite the bullet** and do without a visit at Jack Sharky's place.
But if this was the case, he wanted to have his fun, at least. Justus turned around and speeded up. Perry followed him closely. In this way, he couldn't get rid of him, of course, because the speed was no problem to him. But Justus wanted to **string Perry along** for some more time.
After five minutes though, Justus was out of breath and stopped pedaling. Fortunately, he had just arrived at the entrance of the Rocky Beach City Park. Now Perry had to leave his car. It was a pity that Justus had to get off his bike and push it through the park; otherwise, he would have helped Dick Perry to enjoy an athletic jogging 'performance'. But he wanted to avoid a discussion with the police. Besides, he had a better plan than to get rid of Perry in a wild chase. He pushed his bike into the park. From the corner of his eyes he could see that Perry had parked his car in the no-parking zone and followed him on foot. He was very good at this, always staying within sight and hiding behind other people most of the time.
Justus walked a few more feet, then he sat down on a park

---

lurching, to lurch – schlingern, taumeln; **to bite the bullet** – in den sauren Apfel beißen; **to string so. along** – jmd. hinhalten

bench. He looked at his watch and, without attracting attention, cautiously turned around: Perry took a seat on another park bench next to an older **bum** drinking from a bottle wrapped in a brown paper bag.

That bum reminded Justus of an old friend: corpulent stature, a big head, partly bald-headed, hanging cheeks and eyelids. He could have been Alfred Hitchcock's brother …

Justus took his time looking around. In a good **temper** he watched the pedestrians passing by. A few seagulls had gathered, probably looking for food. Justus remembered that he had taken along with him Aunt Mathilda's lunch pack that he hadn't eaten yet. He pulled it out, took a few big bites, and fed the rest to the birds.

To keep Perry interested, he often looked at his watch and pretended to nervously sit on the edge of the park bench, as if he would wait for someone. Suddenly he discovered Mr. Barnes, his English teacher, amongst the people in the park. His showing up was just perfect. A little conversation with him would strain Perry's nerves even more. Of course, Perry couldn't hear that Justus was talking to his teacher only about trivial things.

Barnes had also recognized Justus and came closer. "You here?"

Justus got up. "Yes, sometimes I like sitting in the park to think about things, Mr. Barnes. Have you already looked over the tests?"

"I just scanned them briefly. Not bad, your essay, that's what I can already say. The ending is a little abrupt, though. If you just wouldn't express yourself in such a complicated way …" The teacher laughed shortly and turned around to continue his walk.

---

bum – Stadtstreicher; **temper** – Laune

"Thank you, Mr. Barnes. Have a nice day!"
Mr. Barnes said goodbye and went on.
Justus sat down again. From the corner of his eye he noticed that Dick Perry kept following up on Mr. Barnes with his **binoculars**. Perhaps he thought Barnes would be a secret informant and wasn't certain now whether to follow him or not. But Perry stayed where he was.
Actually Justus could take a relaxed bike trip back to the headquarters now. Dick Perry wouldn't be able to find Peter and Bob any longer. They could visit Jack Sharky undisturbed. But then Justus had a wild idea. He pulled out pen and paper, turned around several times as if he would check up whether someone was watching him, and in large letters he wrote on the piece of paper:

SECRET MESSAGE
And in small letters behind it: *for the second-best detective of all detectives; it's a pity.*
I can be so mean, Justus thought to himself and grinned. Then he continued writing:
Dear Mr. Perry, actually I wanted to suggest that you take a part of your fee to replace the plastic boat you have destroyed. But now that we have fooled you so nicely I think we're even. You don't owe us anything. Oh yes, I should also mention that we have put aside the Baker case for your sake. But we will take care of Tom Wood with all our strength and ***determination****. After all, his mother has told us to look for him.*

---

binoculars – Fernglas, Feldstecher; **determination** – Entschlossenheit, Bestimmtheit

Justus was in an almost **slaphappy** mood. So he kept on writing:
By the way, if you actually manage to solve the case before we can we will design a new motto for your detective agency. For now, may I offer the following version: 'Die drei ??? are first in the jellyfish chase – and Dick Perry is about to lose the case.' With detectivistic greetings, Justus Jonas, First Detective of die drei ???.
OK. Justus folded the paper together and got up. He looked here and there – just don't exaggerate it, Justus thought –, then he placed the paper in the **knothole** of a park tree. Justus looked around once more, then he grabbed his bike and quickly took off.
Hiding behind a bush, Justus Jonas took his pocket telescope and watched how Dick Perry hastily rushed towards the tree, stretching himself as far as possible so as to get a hold of the paper in the knothole.
He unfolded it immediately. Dick Perry's reaction and facial expression was more than a **compensation** for the destroyed plastic boat and the fact that Justus had **to do without** the visit to Jack Sharky.

Meanwhile, Peter and Bob had a meeting that was much less pleasant. First of all, it took quite a while until they had reached the right area in Santa Monica with their bikes. Finally, they found the house they looked for: a large, noble mansion in a respected quarter. But the place was secured by an iron gate and a high wall surrounding the **estate**. Peter discovered a doorbell

---

slaphappy – übermütig; **knothole** – Astloch; **compensation** – (hier -) Entschädigung, Ausgleich; **to do without sth.** – ohne etw. auskommen; **estate** – Grundstück, Anwesen

and rang it several times, but nothing happened. The two detectives were just about to turn around and leave when the heavy gate opened, all by itself.
The boys got on their bikes and rolled down the 300 feet to the mansion. When they parked their bikes the front door opened.
"Yes?" A man in bathing trunks with a large towel around his shoulders stood in front of them. Water was dripping from his hair; obviously he had just gotten out of his swimming pool. His face looked similar to that of a **Great Dane**: indeed, it was the man shown on the photo.
Bob started stuttering: "We … uh, we …"
"Are you here because of my job ad in the paper? Well, you should read it again: I am looking for a *female* home help, not a male! Men just can't do a proper cleaning job."
"But we …"
"I don't care whose references you're coming up with. And even if it would be the greatest Hollywood director of all times: I don't want male home helps! I had **come a cropper** with such a guy already before. Afterwards my house was sheer chaos. Smeary spots on the window. Water stain marks on the floor. Disorder in my workroom. No, thank you. I'm sorry, guys."
"Yes, then you should really employ a woman," Peter answered when he finally had the chance to answer. "Obviously you've made better experiences with them."
But that seemed to have been the wrong **cue** for Sharky. "Well, you can't really put it that way," the man said. "It's just that there are hardly any good people around anymore these days! My last home help had let me down big time! Me! And I really

---

Great Dane – (Deutsche) Dogge; **to come a cropper** – auf die Nase fallen, reinfallen; **cue** – (hier -) Stichwort

have other things to worry about at this time. It's a pity, because she managed to handle things so correctly and quickly! Well, that lasted for precisely three weeks, then she told me she was overloaded, having to handle a second job as well. And I wouldn't pay her enough. As if the guys at 'Waterworld' would pay her better than me, **fancy that!** That stupid woman prefers this shabby tourist hangout to my beautiful mansion here. She must be out of her mind!"

Sharky's mention of 'Waterworld' made Peter and Bob flinch.

"Mr. Sharky," Bob said cautiously, exchanging a meaningful look with Peter, "that last home help of yours – was the name of that lady perhaps Betty Sutton?"

Just mentioning the name caused a **screaming fit** with Mr. Sharky. "You know this lady? Is *she* sending you?" He held his head. "So that's what it is: you didn't come here to work for me! Rather, you're supposed to pick up her outstanding money, isn't that what you came for? As if you boys would be able to impress me! Oh no, forget it. Go back to your friend and tell her she can say goodbye to her dollars!"

"What are you actually paying per hour?" Bob asked inbetween.

"Enough! Nobody can complain about that! Not even Betty Sutton! Get lost! Or I'll get my gun to convince you that you had better leave!"

He closed the door with a bang.

Bob turned around and was about to leave when Peter held him back. After all, they still had to get a job done. The Second Detective shoved his hand into the back pocket of his trousers. But

---

fancy that! – stell dir das mal vor! **screaming fit** – Wutanfall, Wutausbruch

he didn't find Mr. Sharky's photo there. The other pocket was also empty. "Do you have it?" he whispered to Bob.
"The photo?" Bob stuttered. "Perhaps Justus still has it. Anyway, it's senseless to try to approach this guy with anything. No wonder that all home helps are leaving him. Perhaps he has spent a little too much time in the army."
"I wouldn't like to dust that guy's pictures, either. If he's got any at all, that is."
"But that shouldn't be an excuse for Betty Sutton," Bob continued. "They should actually get along well with each other."
He got on his bike and waited for Peter who, as usual, had locked his bike twice. "All in all, this trip was a big failure," Bob declared. "We couldn't find out anything at all about what Sharky has to hide. Not to mention that we don't have a single trace of Tom."
"That's right," Peter answered and unlocked the second chain, "but Betty Sutton having worked for Sharky, that is more than just pure coincidence!"
Bob nodded. "Indeed, that's something to think about. With these news we might be able to comfort Justus, even though we couldn't find out anything about the photo. Hurry up before this guy shows up again."
But they were able to leave Jack Sharky's ground without further trouble, glad to be back on the road.
On the way back Peter had a hard time to calm down again. "I hate guys like Sharky. Disgusting **know-it-all**. Just think of all those **brainless** remarks he came up with!"
Bob's mood wasn't the best one, either, but when they were heading back to Rocky Beach a sudden smile showed up on his

---

know-it-all – Besserwisser; **brainless** – hirnlos

face. “I just thought of something else, Second. Even if you won’t like it.” With a few strong steps on the pedals, he came closer to Peter.

Peter turned towards Bob. “And what would that be?”

“Kelly,” Bob answered briefly. “She’s a woman.”

“I know,” Peter replied. “From firsthand knowledge.”

“*She* could apply for the job at Sharky’s,” Bob added. “As home help.”

“Are you serious?”, Peter shouted, almost touching a parked car with his bike. “Kelly over at this tyrant’s place? She would never do that. She’s much too **stubborn**!”

“Well, Second, then think of something which might convince your girlfriend,” Bob grinned.

---

stubborn – trotzköpfig, störrisch

A Dog's Breakfast

When Peter and Bob returned to their headquarters Justus was already waiting for them impatiently.

In his usual way Bob summarized what had happened to them. When he mentioned Betty Sutton Justus interrupted him for the first time.

"Betty Sutton has worked as home help for Mr. Sharky? That's one more **indication** that there is a connection between both cases! By all means, we have to find out what exact role Betty is playing in all this."

Peter put up a skeptical face. "Why in the world did she apply for a job with Mr. Sharky? He's really disgusting. Those few dollars she has earned don't make up for having to deal with this sickening fellow! There's more to that here!"

"Best would be, we'd keep her under surveillance," Bob suggested. "Perhaps that trace will lead us to Tom. But I have another idea!" And Bob explained his plan to place Kelly as home help in Mr. Sharky's mansion.

Justus liked the idea at once: "If she works there she could help us sneak into his house secretly and take a good look around. Sharky must have something to do with Tom's disappearance! After all, it was him whose photo was attached to the e-mail. I only hope that we won't have another female applicant getting in our way, **snatching away** the job before Kelly can get it."

"I'm not afraid about that at all. **Considering** the temper of this guy, he's probably going to make every single candidate run at once."

---

dog's breakfast – Schlamassel, Mist; **indication** – Hinweis, Anzeichen; **to snatch away** – wegschnappen, entreißen; **to consider** – nachdenken, überlegen

Justus looked at Peter doubtfully. "Still, Kelly should hurry up. Peter, you tell her. And prepare her well for the job so she knows how to handle this guy; *no* **answering back** or *anything* like that, otherwise the whole plan will **go down the drain**!"
"You mean she should ignore whatever he comes up with and be a nice girl, saying 'yes' to everything?" Peter frowned.
"Wouldn't it be better to ask Bob if Elizabeth could take this on?"
Bob was outraged and wanted to say something in reply, but Justus stopped him. "Elizabeth's nerves are not nearly as strong as Kelly's. To Kelly, this is a child's play. She has managed to handle much tougher stuff."
That was true. In the past, Kelly had once sneaked into a hotel for die drei ??? successfully.
"OK, OK," Peter agreed with a slight grudge. He didn't like it at all to ask Kelly for something. Particularly when it had something to do with die drei ???. She had often complained that Peter would spend more time with die drei ??? than with her. But in the last weeks the relationship between her and the detectives had eased up a lot. Ever since she started to meet with friends on a regular basis to form a beach volleyball group it was Peter who reacted **jealously** toward her frequent appointments.
To loosen things up, Justus told his friends what had happened between him and Dick Perry in the city park. The fact that Perry had simply shot their plastic boat to pieces was something

---

to answer back – freche Antworten geben, widersprechen; **to go down the drain** – in die Binsen gehen, fehlschlagen; **jealously** – eifersüchtig; **to chew on sth.** – an etw. schwer zu kauen haben, etw. in den Knochen stecken haben; **gratification** – Befriedigung; Genugtuung

they still had **to chew on**; thus, Justus's report on how he fooled Perry was met with laughter and **gratification**.
"Pride goes before a fall," Bob remarked.
And Peter summed up: "Sweet revenge!"
Justus grinned. "And another phrase that applies: He who laughs last laughs best!" The three detectives were back in high spirits and called it a day.
It wasn't before noon the next day that they could take up their detective work again. As the day before, Tom's seat in the classroom had remained empty, and die drei ??? were again nervously sitting on the edge of their chairs during class. What was Dick Perry up to in the meantime? Did he already find out about Mr. Sharky and Betty Sutton?
Since their **encounter** in the park they hadn't seen or heard anything of him at all.
When Justus unlocked the door to their headquarters he had an uneasy feeling that he might have been a little too **boastful** in his letter to Dick Perry. Now Dick Perry would do everything to show the detectives that he was the better one. His harpoon shot had demonstrated **vividly** to what lengths he would go to achieve his **ends**. They didn't even want to think about what would happen if Dick Perry would triumph in the end.
When Justus put down his book bag on the desk the phone rang. It was Tom's mother. She sounded very nervous.
"What's new?" Justus wanted to know.
"Tom has just sent me a message," Mrs. Wood hastily answered. "Via e-mail. I shouldn't worry, and he would be back home in two days. I hope so much that this is true!"

---

encounter – Begegnung; **boastful** – überheblich, prahlerisch; **vividly** – eindringlich, deutlich; **ends** – Ziele, Absichten

"Would you please read the whole message to me, Mrs. Wood?" Justus asked.
"'Dear Mom, I know you're worrying about me. But I have to get an important job done. Nothing dangerous or anything to be afraid of. I'll be back the day after tomorrow. So please don't get overexcited. Tom.'"
Justus picked on his lower lip so that his voice didn't sound very clear. "Do you think it was Tom himself who wrote these lines?"
"Pardon me?"
"Would Tom have chosen these words when writing you?"
"You mean whether that's a **genuine** message from him? I don't know. Could be, even though I'm puzzled about Tom's behavior. To the police, it's nothing to really worry about. If he really had been kidnapped someone would have made a claim, be it for money or whatever. Inspector Cotta showed up this morning and also asked me to calm down. What do you think?"
Justus hesitated for a moment. "Perhaps everything is fine," he **reassured** Mrs. Wood. "Uh, one more question: What's the name of the sender of that e-mail? Is it his own?"
"That doesn't work. The address is blocked. He wrote the message from *Bert's Bar*, you know, the café down at the beach."
Justus flinched when he heard Mrs. Wood mentioning Bert's Bar. "I know that place, of course," he quickly answered. "An internet café. Have you already been there before?"
"Of course. But nobody seems to be able to remember Tom having been there. There's just too many people sitting at their computers every day …"

---

genuine – echt, unverfälscht; **to reassure** – beruhigen

Justus thanked Mrs. Wood for the information and hung up. He personally did not believe that it was a genuine message from Tom. The fact that the mail had, once again, come from Bert's Bar seemed to suggest that the mysterious jellyfish **had a finger in the pie**.
And there was something else that worried Justus: Dick Perry. If the detective really wanted to beat die drei ??? then he would install secret listening devices in their headquarters. In this way, he'd be able to find out about the detectives' next steps.
Justus quickly checked whether they had received any unannounced visits. But all their security systems were intact. He also asked Aunt Mathilda whether she had seen anything suspicious, but there was nothing she could come up with.
While Justus took apart the phone to check for any built-in mini microphones Bob arrived. After school he had taken a short trip home before joining his friends at their headquarters.
Bob knew at once what Justus's worried about. "Did this Perry guy actually go so far as to place **bugs** in our headquarters?"
Justus shook his head. "Nothing I could find. Have you heard anything from Peter?"
"No." The Second Detective was on his way with his newly repaired MG to drive Kelly to Santa Monica, applying for the job with Mr. Sharky. It remained his secret how he had managed to get his girlfriend's cooperation. At any rate, he had shown up in school in best spirits and had left for Santa Monica right after school.
After Justus had informed Bob of Mrs. Wood's phone call he went to the computer and turned it on. Perhaps they had re-

---

to have a finger in the pie – die Finger im Spiel haben;
bug – (hier -) Abhörwanze

ceived additional answers to their e-mail campaign. While the computer was starting up Bob was putting the phone together again. His thoughts wandered over to Betty Sutton. What in the world did she want from Mrs. Baker? How did she get to know Sharky? Was *she* the person behind the jellyfish e-mail? Perhaps it was her who had set up the incident with the jellyfish in the boat-wreck. Undoubtedly she was very familiar with these creatures. But at the time those two ladies had been diving Meg Baker's will had not yet been changed. And most of all: had Betty Sutton actually kidnapped Tom because he was hot on her trails? Or was Mr. Sharky behind this? After all, it was him on the photo that Tom had copied.
Once again, his thoughts circled around Tom's puzzle. In it, he talked about *finding HIM*, not *HER*. Didn't that **rule out** Mrs. Sutton? Then he remembered that Tom only knew the e-mail address and not the person behind it. So this didn't give any **clue**, either.
Justus took a look at the computer screen. 'The computer takes a long time to start up today,' he thought to himself for a moment, but he didn't ask himself why. He was too much busy with thoughts leading him once again into the direction of Betty Sutton. When they met her during their visit at 'Waterworld' Betty had this backpack Justus had spilled the water of the bucket over. He remembered that she had a little picture on that backpack. But what did it show? Suddenly Justus saw it clearly before his mental eye: a dog. Dog, dog … Tom's puzzle! It was about *smelling* something! And dogs have an excellent *olfactory sense*! Something seemed to fit together here! Justus be-

---

to rule sth. out – etw. ausschließen, unmöglich machen;
a clue – ein Hinweis

came excited. Dogs exist all over the world, too! That fits as well! Was he close to solving the puzzle? But if that was the case – what was the word they were searching for? Was it the name of a special dog breed? Terrier? Dachshund? Sheltie? There were many possibilities. ' ... *but if you're trying to find HIM, reach beyond your bounds*, Tom had written. What was that supposed to mean within this context?

Suddenly Justus' train of thought was interrupted. His only attention was now devoted to the computer. He stared at the screen. Strange things happened there. A weird sound escaped Justus's mouth.

Bob had just pulled out a new **crate** with **beverages** from the shelf in the back section of their headquarters and turned around **startled**.

"You're OK? Sounds as if you've got with a smoker's lung!"

"Come here and take a look at this!"

Bob dropped the crate and rushed over to Justus.

On the screen they could see three jellyfish slowly moving from one corner to the other. Suddenly a dark rectangle, looking like a slab of chocolate, became visible. One after the other, the three jellyfish started **to eat away at** that rectangle. It went faster and faster.

Bob couldn't take his eyes off the screen. "What the hell are they doing there?" he asked startled.

---

crate – Kiste; **beverage** – Getränk; **startled** – überrascht, verblüfft; **to eat away at sth.** – an etw. nagen, etw. wegfressen

Virus Attack

Justus was **perplexed** and helpless. Meanwhile, the jellyfish had eaten away half of the rectangle. Then **it dawned on him**. "The hard disk!" he shouted. "They are destroying the hard disk of the computer! All our files are at risk!"
Helplessly, Justus pressed a few keys – but with no visible success. With incredible speed, the slab of chocolate disappeared, literally **bit by bit**.
Bob couldn't look at it any longer. He crawled under the desk. "I'll pull the plug," he exclaimed **determined**. "Or? What do you think?"
"Of course, go ahead and try!" Justus answered. "Seems it doesn't matter anyway. Wait … it's too late! Total loss. Everything's gone. The screen is black."
Bob crawled back out from under the table. "And what does this mean, Just? Hopefully not what I'm afraid of?"
"I'm afraid it does! The jellyfish has sent us a computer virus. Everything is destroyed!"
"You mean my complete archive is destroyed as well?" Bob asked. Sheer horror showed up on his face. The work of years had been ruined within a few minutes.
"Yes."
"Our reports, our photos, the fingerprint file, the programs for **deciphering cryptographic messages**, the … the phone directory, my *Deep Space* video game …"

---

perplexed – ratlos, verblüfft; **it dawned on him** – es dämmerte ihm; **bit by bit** – häppchenweise, Stück für Stück; **determined** – entschlossen; **deciphering, to decipher** – entschlüsseln, dechiffrieren; **cryptographic messages** – Geheimbotschaften

"Yes, that one as well. Same with my chess game. Everything we haven't saved to floppy disks is gone."
Saved. Of course. During the first few moments of horror Bob had totally forgotten about it. The complete archive was saved to floppy disks. They still had the original files of most of their games, or they knew at least where to get them. Still it would be a huge effort to get everything installed again.
Justus tried to remember the files they hadn't saved **beforehand**. He turned pale. "All the e-mails of our e-mail avalanche are gone. And Tom's e-mail. I hadn't thought of also saving it to a floppy disk. But I still should be able to remember Tom's puzzle, hold on ..." He took pen and paper and wrote:

It's not an elephant but he's got a big nose
*Every **fug** is known to him, nothing he can't **disclose***
In every country he exists and can easily be found,
*But if you're trying to find HIM, reach beyond your **bounds**.*

"That's the original wording. After all, I've been thinking about it for long enough."
Bob laughed. "You've been thinking about it? And when was that? I think we haven't worked on this puzzle long enough yet."
"In school. During history class."
"And? What's the result?"
"That Tom Wood is a good poet when it comes to puzzles. At least when you think of the short time span in which he managed to think it up. At first, nothing came to my mind, ab-

---

beforehand – zuvor, im Voraus; **fug** – Mief; **to disclose** – aufdecken, enthüllen; **bounds** – Grenze, Rand solutely nothing. But now I believe I've found a trace." Justus told Bob about his idea with the dog. This took Bob's attention off of the incident with the computer. But even with combined efforts they couldn't get any further. Some important **hint** was still missing.

So their **euphoria** quickly disappeared again, and Bob stared back at the black computer screen. He still couldn't believe it.

"How did that virus manage to invade our computer?"

"We activated it ourselves. Usually that happens when you open the e-mail containing the virus. It must have been amongst the answers to our e-mail avalanche. But I'm afraid we won't be able to find out anymore. If I remember correctly Peter had loaded all files up on the computer, and all those files are deleted now."

"Then it follows, you mean, that the jellyfish has ... found out about our e-mail avalanche?"

Justus nodded with a grudge. "I'm afraid that's what it means. Maybe that action was too risky, after all. Let's **assume** that Betty Sutton is actually the person behind the jellyfish. For some reason perhaps, her e-mail address might show up in one of the mail address files of our friends, or their friends in turn, and everything is promptly presented to her on a **silver platter**. Same goes for Jack Sharky." The thought of it drove Justus mad. "I could bite my ... over so much stupidity."

"And what's up with Mrs. Baker? The woman it all started with?" Bob suddenly asked.

"Why Mrs. Baker?"

---

hint – Hinweis, Wink, Tipp; **euphoria** – Hochstimmung, Euphorie; **to assume** – annehmen; **silver platter** – Präsentierteller, Silbertablett

"Perhaps Mrs. Baker is not so **inexperienced**, after all, as she **pretends**, and she herself is behind all this stuff."
"Absurd."
"Remember her password: Harry!"
"So?"
"Her dog's name is Harry!" Bob gasped. Justus still didn't understand. "Just! That fits exactly to the solution of the puzzle, as you yourself assumed! A dog! Even the line ... *but if you're trying to find HIM, reach beyond your bounds"* finds an explanation with this: the solution is right around the corner. We only have to look around!"
"Then the trace must lead us **via** Jack Sharky to Mrs. Baker," he admitted. "But she doesn't have any motive at all! Where's the connection supposed to be? And most of all: do you really believe she could do something like that? Then it would've been a gigantic show she has **staged**!"
"I believe it could be anybody," Bob answered, "unless we can prove the opposite. Isn't that usually *your* motto?"
"Well, yes," Justus had to admit.
The phone interrupted their thoughts. It was Kelly.
"Hi Just! This is Kelly. You can **set out** now! For Jack Sharky's place, that is."
"Kelly!", Justus shouted in surprise. "You're already at his place?"
"Yes, and I can't speak very loudly. I introduced myself to him and he kept me here right away. Oh man, this guy is disgusting! Right now he's sitting out at the pool. He's constantly com-

---

inexperienced – unerfahren; **to pretend** – vorgeben, vorspiegeln; **via so. to so.** – über jmd. zu jmd. anderem; **to stage** – inszenieren, veranstalten; **to set out** – sich auf den Weg machen nach/zu

ing up with new stuff he doesn't like about the world. I have a hard time getting my work done, considering how **fussy** he is. If it weren't for you guys ..."

"How can we get into the house?"

"Just wait in front of the iron gate. I'll open it when I see you. There's an open window on the back side of the house. But for God's sake don't make any noise! And don't you change or move a single thing! This Sharky guy will kill me if he finds out! And hurry up so I don't have to show up here once more. Oh, hold on: you'll have to wait for Peter, of course. But he should be with you any minute."

"Kelly ..."

"I have to end off. Sharky is calling for me again!"

Justus hung up. "Did you get everything?" he asked Bob.

Bob nodded. "That's great. The sooner the better. Just let me quickly fetch our equipment."

They didn't have to wait long. Right when Justus closed the door behind him Peter drove through the front gate of the junkyard with screaming tires. His MG was back in good shape. Uncle Titus came running out of his tool shed, fuming. "I told you not to speed on the junkyard ground, Peter!"

Peter got out and slammed the car door shut. "An emergency, Mr. Jonas!"

"An emergency, yes yes. That seems to apply to your bikes, too," Titus Jonas replied, pointing with his finger to Justus's and Bob's bikes leaning against the wooden fence. All tires were flat, they could see it, even from a distance.

Die drei ??? rushed over to examine the damage. Nails were sticking in every single tire. Then they discovered a piece of

---

fussy – kleinlich, meckernd

scrap paper sticking under one of the **carriers**. "Hello you drei ???," Justus read, "thank you very much for the friendly instructions yesterday in the park. This is to thank you. Greetings, Dick Perry, who will triumph over you guys anyway in the end! – PS: do you know my new motto: Dick Perry's got the **villain** nailed – die ???'s investigations failed!"

"This dickhead!" Bob shouted.

"Seems he's not going to give up that easily," Justus had to admit. He was plagued by his **guilty conscience**. Perhaps he had gone a little bit too far with his letter.

He turned around to Uncle Titus who was still standing in front of his tool shed, looking at the boys in amusement. "Uncle?"

"Yes?"

"Would you do us a big favor and, just this one time, repair ... our bikes ... the tires, that is ...?"

"No way," Titus Jonas was outraged. "That's your own job."

"Uncle, please. We have an urgent appointment," Justus apologized and hastily waved at his friends to come to the car.

---

carrier – (hier -) Gepäckträger; **villain** – Verbrecher, Schurke, Bösewicht; **guilty conscience** – schlechtes Gewissen

Face to Face

In Peter's MG they were much faster in Santa Monica than with their bikes the day before. During the trip Justus and Bob looked through the rear window, time and again, to check whether Dick Perry would be following them. But there was no trace of him.

Die drei ??? found out why that was the case when they turned into the street where Jack Sharky was living: Dick Perry's gray Ford was already parked across from the front gate.

"**Duck**!" Peter shouted just in time.

Bob and Justus dived down, and Peter managed to fold the sunscreen down in front of the **windshield** just in time. Hopefully Dick Perry hadn't recognized them.

Now they couldn't park their car in front of Sharky's estate. It was impossible to hang around in front of the gate until Kelly would be able to open it. Without taking his foot of the **accelerator** Peter kept on driving and didn't stop until he had taken a turn around the corner.

"A punch into the stomach," Bob commented Perry's presence. "So Dick Perry is already hot on Sharky's trails. That was it for a **head start**."

"I hadn't expected that, either," Justus had to admit as well. "Indeed, he's better than we thought."

"But Perry is still waiting in front of the gate, and we're going to be on the other side pretty soon!", Peter tried to lift their mood a little.

---

duck! – (hier -) ducken! **windshield** – Windschutzscheibe; **accelerator** – Gaspedal; **head start** – Vorsprung

Justus laughed bitterly. "Our original plan might have been fine. But now we can't simply march by Perry, tap him on the shoulder, and wish him good luck while we enter Jack Sharky's estate! If he wants to **get even with** us, he could simply ring up Sharky and tell him that there are unwanted visitors on his property. And we can make up our minds how to get out – of prison, that is."

"Kelly could do some searching by herself," Bob suggested.

"Forget it," Peter replied.

Bob remembered that, in any case, they didn't have a chance to contact Kelly anymore. "**Postpone** the action?" he cautiously asked.

"No way," Justus decided. "We'll look for a place where we can climb over the wall. Hopefully Kelly will have opened the window already."

"If I take two more corners we'll get into the little side street next to Sharky's property," Peter explained. "The wall is pretty high, though." But the longer he was thinking it over the more he became worried. "But it wouldn't be a wise idea to climb over the wall; that's burglary! And most of all, we haven't arranged it with Kelly. Just about everything could go wrong."

"Let's still do it, after all," Justus said. "It's for Tom's sake. Let's go."

Not too happy, Peter started the car and drove down two streets until they came up to the little side street next to Sharky's property. A few cars were parked here and there inbetween the trees. Peter parked the MG in a free spot. "Here it should be," he said. "But the wall is still higher than I thought."

---

to get even with so. – jmd. eins auswischen, sich rächen;

to postpone sth. – etw. verschieben, vertagen;

"Seven feet, I guess," Justus said and looked around. "We're lucky that nobody is out on the street."
"But the people from the opposite side of the street could see us," Peter **objected**.
"I don't think they'll be standing behind the curtains, looking out the window all day," Justus calmed him down.
"And what if Perry suddenly turns around the corner and shows up?"
"We'll have to take a certain risk. Come on, park the MG as close to the wall as you can."
Peter moved the car back and forth a few times. Finally, Justus was satisfied. The car was now parking so close to the wall that Bob and Justus had to get out of the car on the driver's side as well. Without attracting attention, the three boys **scrutinized** the surroundings. They couldn't see anybody, and nobody seemed to look out the window of the house across the street.
"And now?", Peter asked.
"It's a pity that your MG is so low," Justus said. "But it might still be enough."
"Enough for what?" Peter looked at him. "You guys don't plan to …?" He turned pale. "So that's why you wanted me to park the car so close to the wall! No way! My beautiful valuable car! Just, this is a very special car and my dearest! Forget about your plans!"
Justus ignored the Second Detective, stepped behind the car, and started to cautiously climb up on the **trunk**.
"My car will never be able to take your weight," Peter was **whining**. "Just, you can't get up there, you're much too heavy!"

---

to object – einwenden, beanstanden; **to scrutinize** – prüfen, untersuchen; **trunk** – (hier) Kofferraum; **to whine** – jammern

"We'll see," Justus replied and placed one knee on the roof. They could hear a slight 'plop'. The **sound set Peter's teeth on edge**. Justus pulled himself up onto the roof of the MG and tried to climb up the wall. Soon he reached its upper edge. He quickly looked over on the other side, and slowly he swung himself over the wall. A dull sound announced his landing in Sharky's garden.

"Well yes," Bob said, stepping from one foot onto the other. "No hard feelings, Peter, but … now that Justus is already … I'm much lighter than him, after all … and it's for Tom's sake, anyway …" He nodded to Peter in an encouraging manner, climbed up onto the car roof – considerably faster than Justus – and quickly pulled himself over the wall, too.

In despair, Peter's hand touched the new **dent** in the body of his car. What should he do? He looked up and down the street, checked the house on the other side, **estimated** the effort to climb over the wall, and followed Justus and Bob.

They were already waiting for Peter behind a bush. "There you are, finally," Justus hissed, "we're lucky. Look! Over there is the open window! And back there in the garden you can see a part of the swimming pool. Seems, Sharky hasn't caught wind of our **intrusion**."

Bent over, he started running; the way to the house went slightly uphill. Bob followed him closely, and Peter didn't have any other choice than to follow them as well.

It was no problem to climb through the window. A few seconds later, die drei ??? were inside the house. They looked around

---

to set so.s teeth on edge – jmdm. durch Mark und Bein gehen; **dent** – Beule, Druckstelle; **to estimate** – einschätzen; **intrusion** – Eindringen, Eingriff

and a smile showed up on their faces: Kelly had helped them to find their way inside the house. They were in the dining room, but an open door showed them that Sharky's workroom was right next door.

"Let's go to work, guys." Justus went ahead on tiptoes. Sharky seemed to have a preference for past centuries. Dark, heavy furniture dominated the room. On one of the walls they saw an oversized painting showing the stormy sea; the **trashy** kitsch image was only **surpassed** by its opulent gold-colored frame. But now was not the time to think about taste. First of all, Justus wanted to get an overview. Cautiously he stepped up to the outer glass door which was framed on both sides by heavy curtains dropping all the way to the floor.

The door led to the streetside and was locked. As the house was placed on a slight elevation Justus could see Dick Perry's gray Ford on the other side of the wall. Perry sat behind the wheel and stared at the front gate. Justus smiled to himself. Now the advantage was theirs again. But so far they hadn't been able to find anything.

Justus scrutinized the room. Jack Sharky had positioned his desk in such a way that he had a free view outside the window while working. The desktop looked chaotic. Letters, slips of paper, books. Certainly there was something to discover here.

Besides the furniture and the desk, there was a shelf overfilled with folders and a massive **cabinet**.

Right next to the desk Sharky had set up his computer on a side table. Of course this attracted Justus's interest, even though it wouldn't be simple get to its information without knowing the password.

---

trashy – Schund-, billig, wertlos; **surpassed, to surpass** – übertreffen, überbieten; **cabinet** (hier -) – Aktenschrank

"What if Jack Sharky catches us here **red-handed**?" Peter whispered. "There is hardly any place to hide!"
"In case of an emergency, Bob and I will slip behind the curtains, and you, Peter, you ... you'll hide in the cabinet!"
"I also want to hide behind the curtains!"
"But only two people can fit behind them."
"And why do *I* have to ... well, never mind." Peter checked the cabinet door. With a **creak** it opened. He was satisfied to see that he'd be able to fit in between the cardboard boxes stacked inside if they really had to hide.
Outside they could hear Mr. Sharky calling for Kelly. "How much longer do I have to wait for my drink? Let's go!"
"Yessir, right away!" Kelly answered. Then they could hear her steps as she ran back and forth.
"I guess the guy will play around in the water for some more time to come," Justus noticed. "Bob and Peter, you check the desk and everything on it, I'll take care of the computer."
Systematically they went to work.
Bob pushed aside the old paperweight, a large glass bowl looking like the Earth. He and Peter examined paper after paper, scanning Sharky's notes.
"Now that's interesting," Peter mumbled after a while and looked up. "Jack Sharky owns five old fish cutters. They're all located in Marina del Rey. He lends them out for private roundtrips."
Interested, Justus looked up from the computer. "Jack owns boats? Perhaps that's a clue. Sorry guys, but I'm still working on the password."
"That's all so far, big detective?" Peter teased him and grinned.

---

red-handed – in flagranti, auf frischer Tat; **creak** – Knarren, Quietschen

"I've tried everything possible. Why don't you read the names of the ships to me?"
Peter looked at the piece of paper again. "Yeah, the names are all here. *Sea Star, Santa Monica III, Janine, Blue Sea, Cutty Sark.*"
"*Cutty Sark*?" Bob interrupted him. "Isn't that the cutter that had sunk recently?"
"Of course, the jellyfish boat Mrs. Baker has been diving down to!"
"Then it's … that's impossible!" Excited, Justus typed the name into the computer.
But sadly, it wasn't the correct password, either. Before Justus could try another spelling of the name they heard steps next door.
"Alarm!" Peter hissed. "Hide!"
It was too late to turn off the computer. Someone was entering the dining room next door. Peter disappeared into the cabinet and pulled the door shut from inside.
Justus and Bob hurried up to hide behind the curtains. Unfortunately, they both chose to hide behind the same curtain. They bumped into each other painfully. "Watch out, Bob!"
"Why me?"
It was too late to change places. Justus pushed himself into the corner as far as possible and pulled Bob up close to him. It wasn't quite enough, though: they could probably still be seen from the side.
Someone entered the room. Die drei ??? held their breath. But suddenly there were no more steps they could hear. Justus felt cold shivers running up and down his back. Had Sharky become suspicious?
It was hard to decide where exactly the person was in the room. Now Justus could hear someone making a sound at the desk.

Then someone typed a few letters on the keyboard. An acoustic signal indicated that the computer had accepted the password. Justus **was scared silly**: it was Jack Sharky. And somehow he had found out that something wasn't right …
A slight **air draft** went through the room. Where was Sharky now? Something clicked. Justus closed his eyes, wishing himself back to their headquarters at once.
Then Justus heard someone breathe. Right on the other side of the curtain, just a few inches away from him.
Face to face, they were standing right in front of each other, Sharky and him! Only the curtain hung between them. Justus held his breath.

---

was scared silly – rutschte das Herz in die Hose;
air draft – Luftzug

Red Alert!

There was only one solution: Justus and Bob had to rip the curtain aside and surprise him. Justus looked at Bob and signalized him what he planned to do. Bob understood the strategy. The First Detective **clenched his fist** to get ready for a good punch, and Bob held on to the curtain.

But right that moment another person was faster than them.

RRIPP!

The curtain was open.

"Uhuhh! Die drei ???," they heard a female voice.

"Goddamnit! Kelly!" Justus could hold back his fist just in time. "You scared us silly!"

"Scared? I believe you're quite happy to see *me* here and *not* Mr. Sharky," she replied. "Where is Peter? I hope he's not running around in the house?"

Justus pointed at the cabinet, the door of which opened that moment. Puzzled, the Second Detective came crawling out from in between the cardboard boxes.

But Kelly almost ignored him. "And now please explain to me why you didn't stick to my plan!" she asked angrily. "You never stick to our agreements! I keep staring towards the gate to see you out there, but you've already started happily scrutinizing Mr. Sharky's workroom! Actually, I had a different idea of our cooperation!"

"Happily? I don't think so," Peter answered meekly. "We had to change our plan and climbed over the wall."

Red alert – höchste Alarmbereitschaft; **to clench one's fist** – die Faust ballen

Bob jumped to his assistance. "It's because there is … well, there's another detective also working on the case, lurking around in front of the gate."
"Another detective?"
"Yes," Peter took over. "A real bugger, a slimy, fat guy, a …" He was searching for words.
"**Mean**," Bob helped him out. "Really mean!"
"And so … slimy!"
"The plastic boat that you gave to Peter as a present – he shot it to pieces with a harpoon," Justus added. "Didn't Peter tell you that?"
"No, so far he didn't."
"I hadn't had the time yet," Peter made excuses. He could have saved himself his excuses, because if it needed anything else to set Kelly up against Dick Perry, then it was the information about the harpoon shot destroying their plastic boat.
Justus had already understood that. "He thinks we're stupid amateurs. He has even tried to take the case away from us. When you leave the house later on he might come up to talk to you, and then it would be best if you'd say …"
"… that you are inside, and he only needs to pick you up right here. Is that what you mean, Justus?" She grinned at him in a provoking way.
"Yes, well no …" He laughed. "Sorry, I know you're not stupid."
"For now, you're right." Kelly had calmed down again. "Okay, you drei ???, I don't think I'll have any problems with this Perry guy. Now go ahead and do your job. By the way, you don't have to search for Tom. I've already searched the whole house.

---

mean – gemein, niederträchtig

Nothing. Okay, I have to go outside again, otherwise Sharky will become suspicious."
Before she left Justus held her back. "How did you get to know the password for the computer?"
"That was irritating to you, wasn't it? Some hours ago, Sharky has typed my address into his file, and while he did I looked over his shoulder, without his noticing it: it's *Doggy*."
After so much help, Peter got back control. Gratefully, he gave Kelly a kiss. "See you later, sweetheart, in case we shouldn't be able to meet here anymore."
She grinned and turned around: "Don't you cause me any further trouble!"
"Did he say *sweetheart*?" Bob asked Justus when she was gone.
"I also had this impression," Justus answered and scratched his neck thoughtfully.
"Sweetheart indeed?", Bob teased him.
Peter lifted the paperweight and made a threatening gesture. "You better beware, otherwise you'll feel this one," he replied with a loud voice and threatened to throw the glass bowl at them. Justus immediately hushed him up, putting a finger at his lips. "Don't be so **oversensitive** all the time, Peter," he hissed.
For a moment they listened up to find out whether anybody would enter the house, but nothing happened. So Justus jumped over to the computer, the password of which he now had. "*Doggy* – another hint at a dog," he mumbled. Somehow it was fitting perfectly to Sharky's brawny face.
He didn't have to search for long. Amongst the mails saved on the computer he found a message, the sender of which was only too familiar to him: "Listen to this," Justus whispered and

---

oversensitive – überempfindlich

bent forward, closer to the screen, "here's a mail from Mrs. Baker. I had a suspicion all that time! Highly interesting what she's writing: *Doggy, I'm sure you're involved in some dirty business again! Since when do you personally take a tour out with your old fish cutter in the midst of the night? No wonder you crashed on the cliffs; I guess you were drunk again. Even if the police wasn't able to find anything – I'll personally take a look at the boat, that you can be sure of! And at some point I'll get you! And then you will finally go to jail. Meg.*"
"Then Sharky is her ex-husband!" Bob exclaimed in surprise. "The guy she was so angry about when we were over at her place. She seems to hate him big time."
Justus nodded. "That explains quite a few things. And that's also why Perry is out there. Mrs. Baker has informed him of her suspicion after she handed him the case."
Peter tried to bring order into his thoughts: "Wait a second, in this message Mrs. Baker announces that she wants to take a closer look at the wreck. And Sharky wanted to prevent that from happening. There was something strange going on that night when he crashed the boat on the cliffs. And his ex-wife wasn't supposed to find out. That's why he organised this jellyfish incident. In this way, he could get even with her."
"Then he must have worked with Betty Sutton," Bob concluded. "But why in the world is he so angry about her then?"
"Camouflage?" Peter suggested.
While they thought it over Justus was searching for an answer Sharky might have written Meg Baker. But he couldn't find any. He clicked through various other files, but only got lost in a number of other sub-files that had nothing to do with the case. Slightly disappointed, he shut down all programs. "Well, we won't be able to look everything through. But I guess we have found enough."

While he shut down the computer the First Detective **summarized**: "Sharky is the ex-husband of Baker. Betty Sutton worked at his place as home help, but at the same time she is a friend of Mrs. Baker. Sharky had steered the boat that had sunk. To Mrs. Baker, it is strange that Sharky himself was navigating the boat, and she accuses him of beeing involved in something illegal, perhaps. She wants to check up on it and dives down to the place where the boat crashed. The jellyfish cause her severe skin burns. **Incidentally**, Betty Sutton has joined her – the same Betty Sutton who is working at 'Waterworld' where they're missing a few jellyfish, again by pure coincidence. As strange as it may sound, but it would fit if Sharky and Betty would work together. It's a pity, though, that I couldn't find a definite piece of evidence on Sharky's computer that he's behind the jellyfish mails. And finally: we still don't have a single trace of Tom."

"We should go and do some searching at Betty Sutton's place," Peter suggested. "For some reason she seems to be at the center of all this." His hand touched the large glass bowl; he seemed to really like it.

At that moment, Bob cleared his throat for all to hear. During the conversation between Peter and Justus he had opened one of the desk drawers and searched around in it a little bit. Very cautiously, he pulled something out. It was a small, shining bar of gold.

"Gold," Peter called out. "And what a big bar!" Fascinated, he turned to Bob. His arm touched the paperweight on the edge of the desk. With a loud crash it hit the floor. Glass **splinters** were now all over the place.

---

to summarize – zusammenfassen; **incidentally** – zufällig; **splinters** – Splitter

"Peter!", Justus shouted.
Bob returned the bar of gold into the drawer and quickly closed it again. "Are you crazy?!"
Startled, Peter stared at the mess, unable to act in any way. His first impulse was to sweep up the splinters, but in their present situation this was nonsense. "I … I …," he stuttered.
Suddenly they heard someone entering the room, and they hastily turned around. They were lucky – it was only Kelly.
"**What the heck** have you done there?" When she saw the damage she was close to **freaking out**. "Sharky just came back into the house; he must have heard the noise! He'll show up in a few seconds!" She looked around. "Hide! Fast!"
Justus and Bob disappeared behind the curtains, while Kelly pushed Peter, still shocked and unable to move, into the cabinet, closing the door behind him. Just in time they were in their hiding places, because the very next moment Mr. Sharky jumped into the room, fuming.

---

what the heck – Was zum Teufel; **to freak out** – ausflippen, die Fassung verlieren

Kelly Gets Kicked Out

Sharky's look was fixed on the floor, full of splinters of glass. "What have you done there, Kelly! You stupid idiot!"
He bent down and picked up a larger piece of glass. "That was a very valuable paperweight! Oh Kelly, you will make up for the damage! And you're immediately fired, of course! Stop! First you'll sweep up the glass! Why do I always have to deal with losers like you?"
"I … I didn't do it **on purpose**," Kelly tried to calm him down. She didn't have any other choice than to **take the rap** for what Peter had done.
"Sweep it up, stupid!"
Kelly went out to get a broom and a shovel. Sharky **paced** the room, fuming. The glass **scrunched** under his flip-flops.
Still hiding behind the curtains, Justus and Bob didn't dare take a breath. Hopefully, Sharky wouldn't start to find out what else Kelly might have touched. He would quickly discover the unwanted visitors.
Finally, Kelly returned and started sweeping up the splinters. She kept talking without interruption to **distract** Sharky from die drei ???. "I just wanted to wipe off the desk, Mr. Sharky, I didn't do it on purpose, this glass bowl was so close to the edge of the desk …"
"What are you talking about? The paperweight stood in the middle of the desk!" Sharky answered back. "What do you

---

on purpose – absichtlich, vorsätzlich; **to take the rap** – etw. ausbaden müssen; **to pace** – auf und ab gehen; **to scrunch** – knirschen; **to distract so.** – jmd. ablenken

want here, anyway? My office is **none of your business**!" Suddenly his voice had a **threatening** undertone. "You were supposed to clean the windows in the bedroom, Kelly," he slowly said. "I think you're nosing around here, aren't you? Are you out to steal something?" Justus and Bob could hear how he opened the desk drawer. A moment later he sighed with relief. Then he discovered the chaos on the desk. "What is this? My papers are all **disarranged** ..."

"I just wanted to wipe off the desk; I was already done with the windows in the bedroom," Kelly quickly tried to defend herself. "Please believe me: I'm not the kind of person sitting around doing nothing and killing time once she's done with the first job! I'm really sorry about your paperweight, but please don't say such nonsense! Go ahead, feel free to search through my bag!"

"That's what I'm definitely going to do!"

Justus realized that Kelly started to get the situation under control, slowly but surely. Still, it was frightening to think about what would happen if Sharky discovered the three boys. That would have consequences.

Kelly also seemed to be afraid of it.

"Okay, Mr. Sharky," she said, pouring the splinters into a bucket. "I've swept up everything. So you want to fire me immediately. OK, I understand that. Please come to the door with me."

"Can't you find the way out by yourself?"

"Please come to the door with me," Kelly insisted with a firm voice. "Otherwise, you might even say in the end that I have stolen something on my way out. Besides, my bag is outside in the hallway. You said you wanted to take a look at it."

---

none of your business – geht dich nichts an; **to threaten** – bedrohen; **disarranged** – durcheinander

"Well alright." Sharky followed Kelly on her way out.
"Now!" Justus hissed and pulled aside the curtain.
Bob ran over to the cabinet. "Peter, come on, get out!"
Peter crawled out. His legs had almost fallen asleep, and he had to stretch them for a moment. In addition, he was plagued by his guilty conscience. "This dickhead is obviously stuck in the last century! Poor Kelly! He has really given it to her! And all that just because of my stupidity!"
Justus didn't disagree. "You can **comfort** Kelly later," he only said. "There's going to be many more long movie nights. But for now, let's get the hell out of here!"
But they didn't get very far. The moment they arrived at the door of the workroom they could hear Sharky returning. And now the phone started ringing, on top of all.
"Back!" Justus commanded. "Fast!"
Just in time, die drei ??? disappeared back in their hiding places. Sharky came rushing in and picked up the phone. "Hello? – Yes, on the phone. Didn't you want to call a little bit later? – Are *you* behind this, Meg? This **disguised** voice! – Yes, yes, OK, OK, I know, you make the rules. – Yes, the gold is here. I took it out of my **safe deposit box** today."
Sharky paused and didn't say anything for a few seconds. Obviously the caller seemed to explain something to him in detail. Justus and Bob stood behind the curtains and listened up.
"Yes, I got it," they could hear Sharky again. "OK, in an hour. Yes, I'll be there on time! – Via e-mail? Now?"
Sharky turned on the computer. For one minute, they could only hear the sound of the computer starting up. "Yes, the mail

---

to comfort – trösten; **disguised** – verstellt, verschleiert;
safe deposit box – Schließfach

has arrived," Sharky said. "Wait a second, I'll take a look at it. – Yes, I know the place you mean. – Yes, of course, I'll be there! But I'll get the goods! – Listen, I must be able to rely on that! What else would be my guarantee? – Yes, yes, I'll do as you say!"
Mumbling something to himself, Sharky banged the phone receiver back into the cradle. They could hear that he was printing out something. He folded the piece of paper together, then he opened the **drawer** of his desk. A few seconds later he left the room. He hadn't turned off the computer. Shortly after, they could hear the front door opening and closing.
Suddenly, die drei ??? were alone in the house.
With a sigh of relief, Justus and Bob pushed aside the curtain. Justus walked up to the glass door and could see how Perry's gray Ford started to move so as to follow up on Sharky.
"Now it's Perry's turn," Justus remarked. He didn't like that idea at all. The First Detective could feel that he was nervous. That didn't happen so often; most of the time, he turned as cold as ice in dangerous situations, with his mind speeding up to top performance. But the strange call they had overheard was the beginning of something important, and Justus couldn't find the solution to it. But the fact that Dick Perry was now very close to solving the case was too much for him. Time was running out for die drei ???.
Justus turned around. Helpless, Peter and Bob stood in the middle of the room and waited for the First Detective to come up with a bright idea. "By the time we get to the car Sharky will be miles away," Justus said. But then he remembered the computer. "He had printed out something, right?"

---

drawer – Schublade

While Justus took care of the computer Bob checked the drawer and noticed that Sharky had taken the gold along with him. Justus checked the e-mail in-box. "The last mail is from the beach café! You remember, the camouflage address. Wait, I'm going to open the attachment. Well … now that's a surprise!"
Die drei ??? stared at the screen. The document that showed up there was only too familiar to them. It was the drawing Tom had sent them in an e-mail.
"This treasure map with those lines again – now what is it supposed to mean?" Justus mumbled.
Peter didn't have a clue, either. "And why does Sharky receive it as an e-mail? So far, our idea was that he is behind this himself. But then it would be illogical that he …"
"But Sharky isn't totally clean, either," Bob pointed out. "He's up to his neck in trouble. If I interpret the phone call correctly he's being **blackmailed**. At least, he needs the gold to exchange it for some goods. And he doesn't know who he is dealing with. He even suspected his ex-wife to be behind it, our Mrs. Baker." Bob looked up triumphantly. "I told you guys from the beginning, I believe she has a finger in the pie. That also explains her mail to Sharky."
"Illogical," Justus answered back. "I still believe Betty is involved in this. But we don't have to take any further guesses when we follow Sharky. This map here is the key: Sharky had printed it out and said something like 'I know that place'. So it's a **location plan**! But what exactly is the location? If we solve *that* puzzle, we're back in the game!"

---

to blackmail so. – jmd. erpressen; **location plan** – Wegbeschreibung, Lageplan

"So that's where the **handover** is supposed to happen," Bob said. "And that'll be in an hour!"
"In 52 minutes, to be precise," Justus corrected him, looking at his watch. "The map," he said, "focus your attention on the map. It must be somewhere in the northern part of the greater Los Angeles area. A place one can get to easily within one hour. What does this map show?"
"**Hiking trails** in the mountains? The city park?" Peter guessed.
"No, the park has got more than one entrance. Come on, let's hear some more ideas. Otherwise this stupid Dick Perry has got it made." Justus's brain was blocked. He looked at his watch again. "Come on! Hurry up!"
"Why us?" Bob turned around and looked out the window. Justus' hectic behavior made him totally nervous. "Why do all paths on this map just end?" Bob mumbled to himself. "Why all these **dead-end streets**? They don't seem to lead anywhere … Or is it a wall? Some barrier? A borderline?"
Suddenly, Justus tapped his forehead with his hand. "Oh Bob! What would we do without your questions? You're a genius. That's exactly what it is! Of course they're all dead-end streets. They all lead … down to the ocean!"
"The ocean? Of course: the bays! Near the reef! We've been there ourselves!"
They took a close look at the screen. "Wait, this fits exactly! If this is the way down to the cliffs, here, the first turnoff, then it goes on here" – Bob's finger moved along the lines and finally pointed to the marked spot – "then this here must be the small

---

handover – Übergabe; **hiking trails** – Wanderwege;
dead-end streets – Sackgassen

bay from which we swam to the reef. That's the meeting point! Wow! This puzzle is solved!"

"**Let's hit it**," Justus said. "We should be able to make in time."

But Peter didn't move an inch. "We should contact Inspector Cotta and inform him," he pointed out. "We need support. Before that's arranged, I won't go."

"Then give me the car keys," Justus hissed at him.

Peter shook his head and turned around to Bob for help.

Bob answered his look with a **wink** and tried it the rational way: "Just, forget our duel with Dick Perry for a moment," he said calmly. "This is all about Tom. And this Sharky guy is dangerous. We call Cotta. **Period**."

"From here? We can still call him from somewhere else!"

"There's no telephone up on the cliffs."

"Okay", Justus **gave in**. Peter and Bob sharing the same opinion was something he couldn't **neglect** or do anything against. Besides, they were right. "I'll send him a mail with the map as attachment. In this way, he also has the location plan."

Then the three detectives dropped everything, and off they were on their way to the coast.

---

let's hit it – auf geht's, nichts wie hin/weg; **wink** – Zwinkern; **period** – Punkt, aus! **to give in** – nachgeben; **to neglect** – vernachlässigen

Out for a Dive

A look at the watch showed Justus that they had made it just before the hour was up. There were only a few cars in the little parking lot near the rocky coast. Inspector Cotta's car was nowhere to be seen. "What if Cotta is reading the e-mail too late?" Bob asked.

"There is nothing we can do about it anymore at this time," Justus replied. He looked over the parked cars. "Over there is Sharky's car," he pointed out. "And here, a respectful distance away, Dick Perry. We hit the jackpot!"

Both cars were empty. "Come on, hurry up," Justus called the other two detectives. "The next minutes will decide everything!"

The path down into the small, hidden bay was familiar to them; they didn't need a map. There were not many people around here who knew the **shortcuts**. But the three boys had been around Rocky Beach ever since they were small children, and secret hidden bays always had something **enticing** to them. They followed the path, pushed aside a few bushes, and climbed down to the seashore between the **rock spurs**.

The closer the three detectives came to the beach the more they slowed down. Finally, they stopped short when Justus raised his hand.

"Attention! Careful, otherwise we might make a bad mistake!"

They could hear the ocean waves rolling in on the shore. The sun was already close to the horizon, and a slight wind had come up.

---

shortcuts – Schleichwege, Abkürzungen; **enticing** – verlockend, verführerisch; **rock spurs** – Felsvorsprünge

"They must be out here somewhere. Wait." Slowly, Justus **squeezed** himself **by** the rocks, behind which the path led down the last few feet to the shore.
But all of a sudden he pulled back. "Dick Perry is hiding behind a bush about 25 feet away," Justus hissed. "He has chosen the ideal position to be able to watch Sharky. Be quiet, by all means! Why does this guy always have to stand in our way?"
"Because he's smarter than you, Just."
"Are you serious?"
Peter laughed quietly. "**Just kidding**."
"Could you take a look over the bay?" Bob wanted to know from Justus.
Justus shook his head. "Not from this position. We have to get back a little bit and climb up the **headland**."
Carefully, they turned around again. A few feet further down they managed to reach a rock plateau, without being noticed, from where they could observe the bay. But here they were a little farther away from the scene of the events.
Sharky stood at the beach and stared out on the ocean. He was alone.
Justus followed the direction into which Sharky was looking. His attention was attracted by the cliff where the cutter had crashed. Its mast stood out above the water surface; obviously the drift had lifted the boat up again.
"Not a single soul. I'd really like to know who Sharky is supposed to meet here," Bob wondered.
He turned around and looked up the path they had taken down to the bay.

---

to squeeze oneself by sth. – sich an etwas drücken/pressen;
just kidding – nur ein Scherz; **headland** – Landzunge

"The **blackmailer** must be showing up with a boat," Justus **concluded**. "I can't imagine that he's going to take the risk to show up from the landside. But there's no boat. I can't see anything behind the cliff on the ocean, either."
They searched the horizon for anything suspicious. In the far distance two yachts were sailing, but they didn't seem to come closer. "Perhaps Sharky was **lured** into a trap," Justus wondered.
But suddenly Bob picked on the sleeve of the First Detective. "Look, something's happening down there."
Sharky had bent down. He seemed to pull something out of the water; it looked like a long piece of wood. "Do you have your telescope with you?" Justus asked.
Bob pulled the object out of his jacket.
"Come on, give it to me," Justus said. He pulled out the telescope, laid down flat on his **belly**, and supported his arms on a flat rock. In this way he had a better sight. "That's not a piece of wood," he said. "It's a little **submarine**."
"A submarine?"
"Yeah, obviously steered by **remote control**. Like a big toy. Right now, Sharky is pulling out a piece of paper from it and reads it. Now he reaches into the pocket and ... pulls out a gun. Oh man, he's got a gun with him! He lays it down, and now he pulls out the bar of gold. He places it in the submarine, closes the cover, and looks around. Now he takes the boat and walks down a few feet into the water ..."
"I can see it, too!"

---

blackmailer – Erpresser; **to conclude** – folgern, überlegen, schließen; **to lure** – (an)locken; **belly** – Bauch; **submarine** – Unterseeboot; **remote control** – Fernsteuerung

"… and lets it go. It starts. And dives down. I can still see it. **Ingenious**. Absolutely ingenious, I have to admit! The blackmailer sends a submarine. He himself doesn't show up at all! Mr. Invisible has got us fooled! Sharky, Dick Perry and us – we're all **left out in the cold**."
"But where's the blackmailer?" Bob asked. "He must be picking up the gold somewhere, after all!"
"Probably underwater," Justus answered while he was carefully searching the water surface for suspicious air bubbles. "It's a pity that we don't have our diving equipment with us." He laid the telescope aside. "I can't see anything. The sun's **glare** on the water surface is too strong."
"It must be the sunken fish cutter," Peter suddenly said. "The diver is waiting at the cutter! When I was in there I had seen some kind of box! For sure the submarine was in there. Perhaps I ... I could … swim out there. Not too close, of course. Just to take a look who it is."
Justus and Bob looked at the Second Detective in surprise. "What's the matter with you? Aren't you afraid?"
"I still have to **make up for** the glass bowl I had dropped," Peter said quietly. "And I want to know for sure now. Otherwise the blackmailer might escape us in the end. And Tom might be lost forever without a trace."
Justus and Bob exchanged a look.
But Peter kept on talking. "Watch out, I'll climb over on the other side of the rock so that Sharky can't see me. Then I'll swim out from there. I can hold my breath for quite some time. I

---

ingenious – genial; **left out in the cold** – in die Röhre gucken;
glare – grelles, blendendes Licht; **to make up for sth.** – etw. wieder gutmachen, ausgleichen

don't need to come up for air more than four or five times, then I'll be at the cliff. If we're lucky nobody will notice me."
"But by then the blackmailer will be miles away!" Bob objected.
"I don't think so. Look, Sharky is still there. He doesn't have his goods yet."
"**Cash in advance**," Justus added. "He's got rid of the bar of gold. I wonder if he'll get what he came for."
Peter handed Bob his wallet and the car keys. "You hold on to this!" He took off his clothes and dropped them right where he was, leaving only his underpants on. His look was not so **determined** anymore, though, by the time he started climbing down the rocks. Fortunately, the **surf** wasn't that strong so that he could glide down into the water without problems.
"I hope this will turn out all right," Justus mumbled when Peter waved at them once more.
The Second Detective swam a few strokes. When he was up to the headland he took a deep breath and dived down.
Sharky was still staring at the water. Something had to happen soon, otherwise he would see Peter coming up for air somewhere. Undoubtedly Sharky would assume that *he* would be the blackmailer. Justus didn't dare imagine what would happen then.
Nervous, the First Detective picked on his lower lip. Dick Perry was still hiding behind a rock. At least *he* wouldn't be able to discover Peter.
Justus took the telescope again and watched Sharky who was nervously pacing the beach. "Bob, do you see Peter?" Justus asked without taking his look off Sharky.

---

cash in advance – Vorauskasse; **determined** – entschlossen;
surf – Brandung

"He's coming up for air right now for the first time."
"Dammit!"
But right that moment Sharkey's attention got distracted. The submarine showed up again. **Impatiently**, he stepped into the water up to his hips and pulled it ashore. Now he focused his attention back out on the ocean, but it was already too late to discover Peter. Then he opened the cover of the submarine. Justus held his breath.
Sharky took out a little bundle and unfolded it. The contents were glittering in the evening sun. Gold, silver, **gemstones**. It was jewelry.
"Now it dawns on me," Justus said. "If we get Sharky we're going to do Inspector Cotta a big favor."
"And Peter?"
They turned around. Suddenly they could hear another sound besides the gentle rolling of the waves. A diver had come to the surface. With several fast strokes he came swimming up to the shore. That had to be the blackmailer! Obviously he tried to reach the neighboring bay to escape from there.
Justus looked at him with the telescope: but the diver was wearing a mask and he couldn't see who it was.
The First Detective laid the telescope aside and saw the reason for the escape: some distance behind the diver Peter was swimming after him, and he came closer and closer.
Meanwhile, Sharky had also noticed the two. He took his gun, raised it, and aimed at them. But then he seemed to think again. Quickly, he stuffed his gun back into his pocket and climbed up the rock from where he could look into the neighboring bay.

---

impatiently – ungeduldig; **gemstones** – Edelsteine

Justus saw Dick Perry leaving his hideout and following them. He didn't really have to careful not to be seen. Obviously, Sharky had only one thing in mind: to catch the blackmailer. Justus folded the telescope together and put it back into the jacket. "Now we have to be fast, Bob."

Perry Strikes Hard

"What if Sharky thinks that Peter is working with the blackmailer?" Bob asked when they were sliding down the rocks to follow up on them.

"Then he's going to have a hard time."

"We must warn Peter or stop Sharky!" the First Detective replied.

When Justus and Bob jumped down onto the bottom of the small bay there was no trace of Sharky and Dick Perry anymore. Nervous, Justus looked up the rock. "Cotta, where in the world is Inspector Cotta?!"

Although they were pretty much out of breath already they immediately started to climb up the next rock.

A few moments later they had reached the top from where they could take a look into the next bay.

Justus and Bob held their breath.

Peter had almost caught up to the diver. It was a woman who took off her **fins** in the shallow water and hasted the last few feet towards the beach. In panic, she turned around to the person following her. But the diving mask covered her face.

Peter was already close up to her. Now he had reached the beach as well. The woman started running and headed for the path leading up to the plateau.

Peter had just reached the beach when a sharp call was cutting through the air: "Stop! Both of you! Otherwise I'll shoot!"

Behind a rock, just a few feet away from the woman, Sharky appeared and threatened the woman and Peter with his gun.

---

fins – Flossen

They both stopped in their tracks. Sharky laughed meanly. His gun wandered back and forth between both of them. “Nice couple I’ve caught here. The only thing nicer are those bathing trunks you’re wearing there, boy!”
Peter looked down to his **soaking** wet underpants and decided that it would be better not to answer back.
“Hey, I know you!” Sharky shouted furiously. “Aren’t you one of these guys who were asking about the cleaning job? So that’s what it is: you guys are working together! Give me the gold!”
“But where should I …”, Peter shrugged helplessly. Sharky noticed that Peter wasn’t wearing anything besides his underpants, so he turned towards the woman who hadn’t moved an inch so far. “Well, then I guess *you* are in possession of the bar of gold, sweetie! And take off your mask. I recognize you anyway, Meg! Hand me the gold or I’ll kill you both!”
Justus flinched. Sharky was extremly angry, to say the least. As **short-tempered** as they had known the man, they couldn’t **rule out** that he was deadly serious about it.
Peter began stuttering. Justus had to do something to confuse Sharky. He was just about to scream for a second when Bob pulled on his sleeve and pointed downward. Sharky hadn’t noticed that Dick Perry had approached him from behind. Now he was ready to jump.
Sharky aimed at Peter. “Come on now! One, two …”
Right that moment a hard **blow** hit Sharky’s hand. The gun fell to the ground. Perry grabbed Sharky and made him lose his balance. The detective from Santa Monica knew his business. Al-

---

soaking – klatschnass; **short-tempered** – leicht aufbrausend, reizbar; **to rule out** – ausschließen; **blow** – (hier -) Schlag

though Sharky was physically much stronger than him, Perry managed to put him in handcuffs within a few seconds.
Sharky laid on the rocky ground and was **swearing**.
Justus saw the situation with mixed feelings. "Now we even have to be thankful to this stupid detective," the First Detective mumbled and started moving.
Bob didn't care. Main thing was that Peter was rescued.
But for a second nobody had taken notice of the diver. She wanted to take the opportunity to escape without attracting attention. Justus noticed it first. " The blackmailer! She's taking off!"
Dick Perry grabbed his gun. "Stop it or I'll shoot!"
But unaffected by Perry's threat, the woman kept climbing up the cliff. Obviously she didn't care at all anymore. "Goddamnit!" Dick Perry shouted and began to climb after her.
Quickly, Justus estimated her **escape route**. "We can take a shortcut over the **ridge**," he prompted Bob. "Then we'll get her. Even before Perry!"
The woman realized that she was heading straight for a trap. She slowed down more and more; probably her strength was leaving her by now, too. Halfway up the cliffs she finally gave up.
But this time Justus wanted to be first. Without paying attention to his clothes he worked himself forward. Rocks and stones rolled down under his feet, the knees of his pants were already ripped. Bob had a hard time to follow him.
From below Dick Perry approached the scene, driven by **ambition** just as Justus was.
It was close. Very close. But the little detective from Santa Monica was faster in the end. Exactly one step before Justus he

---

to swear – (hier -) fluchen; **escape route** – Fluchtweg;
ridge – (hier -) Bergrücken, Kamm; **ambition** – Ehrgeiz

walked up to the woman and put his hand on her shoulder. "Dick Perry, Detective Agency Santa Monica. I'll hand you over to the police now … Mrs. Betty Sutton!"
"Betty Sutton?" Bob asked surprised. He had managed to catch up with the small group in the meantime.
Justus nodded silently.
Perry's eyes were glowing. "Yes, this is Betty Sutton, indeed, you super detectives! I've beaten you! I've caught both Sharky and Betty." With a quick grip he pulled the diving mask off the woman's face.
"I hate detectives," Betty said and spit on the ground.
Dick Perry was triumphing. He opened the side pocket of her diving-suit and pulled out the little bar of gold. The gold was shining, reflecting the last few rays of the evening sun. Perry smiled and stuffed the bar into his pocket. "So that's what all the excitement is about! The bar must be worth quite a bit!" He nodded towards Betty Sutton. "OK now, let's go down to Sharky!"
Sharky was still sitting on the beach, guarded by Peter who was shivering from the coldness.
"Betty Sutton!" Sharky hissed. "This **sly cow**! I would never have guessed that! I should have killed you!"
Dick Perry made a **soothing** gesture. "Just come down, Jack. You're up to your neck in trouble yourself! But there's still one question unanswered." He turned around to Betty. "Where are you hiding Tom? In your apartment, perhaps?"
"I'm not going to say anything," the woman answered stubbornly.
The longer Perry was talking the more he got to Justus's nerves.

---

sly cow – raffiniertes Luder; **soothing** – beruhigend

The First Detective had come just as far with his investigations as Dick Perry. But it was a pity that their competitor from Santa Monica had been faster than them in the end. Justus, however, wanted to show that he was up-to-date with the investigations as well, and when Perry paused for a second he spoke up.

"That was a very bad game, Betty," he began with a firm look at her. "As home help you sneaked in at Mr. Sharky's place. He owns five old fish cutters he is renting out. He can't earn very much money with it. But he lives in a luxurious mansion. Somehow that doesn't fit together, you thought, and soon you had found out about his secret: Sharky is engaged in some illegal **delivery** services in exchange for very much money. He takes stolen jewelry and carries it out onto the ocean where he hands it over to other helpers. They, in turn, take the goods offshore and, most probably, carry them **abroad**. Inspector Cotta has told me about the many spectacular thefts that recently happened in the greater Los Angeles area."

"The police will catch the whole gang now," Perry added with a smile. "Which shouldn't be too hard anymore, because you, Mr. Sharky, finally got caught."

"But one day one of your delivery trips failed," Justus continued. "In storm and heavy weather you hit the cliff. The *Cutty Sark* sank and you were hardly able to rescue yourself."

"But the jewelry had sunk with the boat," Perry added. "When you went out the next day to get it someone else had already been faster."

Justus pointed at Betty. "Mrs. Sutton, that is. She dived down to get a hold of the jewelry. But of course she couldn't do any-

---

delivery – Lieferung, Zustellung; **abroad** – (im, ins) Ausland

thing with it as the goods were stolen. She didn't know what to do with it. So she blackmailed you, Mr. Sharky: jewelry for gold. In this way, she had even more in her hands than just a photo she took of you when you entered your boat with a suitcase full of jewelry."
"Gangs of thieves whose **loot** disappears in the ocean can become very mean," Perry continued with a critical look towards Justus.
"But Betty had a problem as well," Justus kept on talking. "Its name was Meg Baker, Sharky's ex-wife. She also knew about the dirty business Sharky was involved in. She was not supposed to get in Betty's way."
"Exactly," Perry interrupted Justus whose explanations obviously went too far for him. "Betty, you made friends with Mrs. Baker. You arranged the jellyfish incident to put pressure on Mrs. Baker. She was supposed to stay away from the sunken boat which was your basis for the money handover."
Justus had taken a deep breath. "I even assume, Mrs. Sutton, you put together one thing with the other and wanted to appear to come to Mrs. Baker's rescue. Of course, you thought, Mrs. Baker would show her gratitude and, in return for your favor, would hand a part of her **inheritance** down to you. Well, it almost worked out!"
Betty turned away. "This detective **babble** drives me up the wall! Two of you wise guys is just too much!"
"I don't think so," Sharky answered back and gave the woman a **fierce** look. "Some parts of what was just said are very interesting! But what about the boys? Were they not part of it?"

---

loot – Beute, Raubgut; **inheritance** – Erbschaft, Nachlass;
babble – Geschwätz; **fierce** – böse, grimmig, verbittert

"We are also detectives," Peter explained, still shivering.

"Actually we're looking for Tom Wood," Justus continued. "Another victim of Betty Sutton. Because there was something else that went wrong: our classmate Tom managed to log in to the computer of Mrs. Sutton. Once logged in, he found files that showed Mrs. Sutton's blackmail activities. But Betty noticed the unwanted electronic visit. Somehow she managed to trace the message back to the sender and identified Tom. She drove to his place, took the files along with her and kidnapped the boy." He looked Betty Sutton directly in the eyes. "Where is Tom, Mrs. Sutton?"

"I'm not going to say a single word without my lawyer!"

"You don't have to ...," Dick Perry began.

"... because we can explain everything," Justus completed the sentence. He smiled triumphantly. "We'll simply take a trip to your apartment, and I'm sure there's something to discover there."

Betty was fuming.

"Go ahead, boys," Dick Perry said, with a look towards Betty. "I believe you're going to find him there. But for now let me make one thing very clear: I, Dick Perry, have solved the case. Even if you were pretty good with your combinations. Maybe one day you might even become a real professional detective. Well, anyhow. *If you need assistance and you're in doubt, call Dick Perry – he'll help you out, after all!*"

He laughed and looked around, but nobody else seemed to share his humor. Perry shrugged and continued: "Tom's rescue, I'll leave that up to you. And turning this fellow over to the police as well." He pointed at Sharky. "But Mrs. Sutton, the actual **culprit**, will be escorted to the police by me personally."

---

culprit – Täter(in)

"Inspector Cotta should be here any minute," Justus pointed out.
"Cotta? Rocky Beach?" Dick Perry made a **disgusted** grimace. He looked as if he had just taken a big bite out of a sour lemon. "No, no, forget it, boys: Santa Monica is the place of the show. I'm working closely together with Inspector Taylor there. Your little nest is not going to win this day, I'm sorry."
He took his gun and pushed Betty Sutton forward. "Let's go, lady, there's the car. Come on, speed it up!"

---

disgusted – angewidert, abgestoßen

The Solution to the Puzzle

Not very happy, die drei ??? watched how Perry and Betty Sutton left. Dick Perry's slogans and wisdoms were hard to take. "He can **spare himself** his arrogance towards Rocky Beach," Justus was **ranting**. He was completely outraged that the detective from Santa Monica had won the race. Tom still hadn't been found yet, and that's what they had to take care of next. Bob had thought of Tom, too, but he had a different question in mind: "What's up with Tom's puzzle? How does that fit with Betty Sutton?"

Peter **moaned**. "Do we really have to solve that right now? I'm freezing!" The wind from the ocean had become stronger, and Peter was a shivering mass of **goose bumps**. "Wasn't it possible for you to take my clothes along, at least?"

Bob looked at him **sympathetically** and pulled off his T-shirt. "Here, put on this one for now. I suggest we climb up to the parking lot and wait for Cotta. In the meantime I can get your clothes. If the inspector still hasn't shown up by the time I'm back we'll take Mr. Sharky to the police station ourselves."

Peter and Justus agreed. "Let's go, Mr. Sharky!"

It took a while until die drei ??? finally arrived in the parking lot with Sharky. Dick Perry had taken off long since. Peter's MG and Sharky's car were the only ones left in the little parking lot. The sun had gone down, and the wind became stronger.

---

to spare oneself sth. – sich etw. sparen, auf etw. verzichten; **to rant** – schimpfen, sich ereifern; **to moan** – stöhnen, ächzen; **goose bumps** – Gänsehaut; **sympathetically** – mitfühlend, verständnisvoll

They placed Sharky on the back seat of the MG and Peter sighed with relief when he took the driver's seat.

Right the moment he wanted to remind Bob to pick up his clothes he saw the headlights of a car cutting through the **dusk**.

"That could be the inspector," Peter hoped. He didn't trust Sharky and wanted to get rid of him as soon as possible.

Between the hills a car showed up. Slowly it came along the sandy road.

Peter breathed a sigh of relief. Indeed it was Cotta's police car. The wheels scrunched on the sand when the car took a turn, headed exactly for Peter, and stopped.

Cotta got out. It was only too visible that he was in a bad mood. "I hope you have a good reason why you called me! We just caught one of the guys of the jewelry gang! I have to question him urgently!" Then he discovered Sharky on the back seat of the car and fell silent.

Justus moved off the **fender** of the MG he had leaned against. At least he could announce one success now. "That fits perfectly, Inspector! Because we're able to present you the messenger who had passed on the stolen goods: Mr. Jack Sharky from Santa Monica! With one of his cutters he took the jewelry offshore. Some extra money, so to speak, in order to secure his lifestyle."

"Really?" Curious, the inspector stepped closer to take a look into the car. "Get out of the car!" He turned back to Justus. "What trace has led you to this guy?"

While Sharky squeezed himself out of the car in a complicated way Justus summarized what they had found out.

"So Betty Sutton has kidnapped Tom!" Cotta realized surprised.

---

dusk – (Abend)Dämmerung; **fender** – Kotflügel

"And I thought the boy had simply run away from home!"
Justus shook his head. "The mail from Tom to his mother was a fake. Betty wanted to **keep** the police **at bay** – which she successfully did."
"And where is this Mrs. Sutton now?" Cotta wanted to know.
"Dick Perry is taking her to the police station in Santa Monica," Justus said a little meekly. "He had caught her first. We still have to free Tom."
"Then Dick Perry **outplayed** you?" Cotta wondered. "Well yes, it is a little surprising that Dick Perry, after a long series of flops and failures ... I had asked some of my colleagues in Santa Monica ..."
In the meantime, Sharky had placed himself next to Cotta. "What is this all about?" he asked with a bad temper. "Is this supposed to be a **stand-up party**? Am I arrested or what? Wouldn't you like to read my rights to me, officer? And then I'll tell you the truth about these three detective **snoopers**. They had tried to creep into my house. **Disguised** as home helps!"
"*Inspector* Cotta," was Cotta's cool reply. "Not *officer*. I'll inform you of your rights on the way back. And I'll talk to Justus, Bob and Peter as long as I please, you got that?" He pointed at the MG. "Why isn't Peter getting out of the car?"
"His outfit isn't quite up to standards," Bob explained. "Perhaps we can talk about the details at the police station. But first we should stop by Betty Sutton's apartment. I think that's the most urgent thing to do now."

---

to keep so. at bay – sich jmdn. vom Hals halten; **to outplay so.** – jmd. übertrumpfen, besiegen; **stand-up party** – Stehparty; **snoopers** – Schnüffler; **disguised** – getarnt, verkleidet

Justus cleared his throat. "No, Bob, we're changing our plans!" he said determined. Bob frowned. What was the matter with the First Detective? Suddenly he appeared completely changed. Justus stepped up to Mr. Sharky and pushed him in the direction of the police car. "Inspector, take care of this guy. We're not driving to Betty Sutton's place. Our **destination** is the harbor of Marina del Rey. Hurry up, Inspector! Every second counts!"
Inspector Cotta looked at Justus in surprise. He was used to quite a few things the boy used to come up with, but this now ...
Justus forced himself to stay calm. "Trust me, Inspector. I'll be able to explain everything later on." He squeezed Bob on the back seat of the MG and slid on the front passenger's seat himself. "**Step on it**, Peter. We're driving ahead. The harbor. Marina del Rey!"
Puzzled, Peter started the car. Slowly, it went along the sandy street. "Am I your taxi?" the Second Detective protested.
"Faster, faster," Justus shouted at him.
Peter didn't react. "Hey listen, you've already done enough damage to my car! Am I supposed to ruin my **shock absorbers** as well now?"
"Come on," Justus said, "it's for Tom's sake!"
Peter speeded up. "If you keep so silent, First, you will not be able to count on me."
"First of all, take the road along the coast. Then we'll see."
A short time later they rushed down the road with the highest

---

destination – (hier -) Ziel(ort); **step on it!** – Gib Gas!
shock absorbers – Stoßdämpfer

speed allowed. Bob thought Justus should now let them in on his plan: "Come on, give us a clue!"
"The puzzle," the First Detective answered.
"What puzzle?"
"Tom's puzzle." He closed his eyes and mumbled:
"It's not an elephant, but he's got a big nose,
Every fug is known to him, nothing he can't disclose,
In every country he exists and can easily be found,
But if you're trying to find HIM, reach beyond your bounds."
Bob shrugged. "So? We were following this dog trace, it has something to do with Betty's backpack. Perhaps she's also running an internet homepage named after a dog breed, or something like that. Hey Just, I don't know."
Peter had to brake as they were passing through a little village. Then he speeded up again. "You mean the dog trace is wrong?", he asked Justus and looked into the **rearview mirror**. In the far distance inspector Cotta showed up.
"Exactly."
"What else did we have …" Bob asked. "Rats, elephants, skunks …"
"No animals," Justus helped them. "Only **in the figurative sense**."
"Fug, perfume, **septic tanks** …" Peter **swerved** to the side to avoid a crash with a motorcyclist. They had reached the city limits of Santa Monica by now. Marina del Rey wasn't too far away anymore.

---

rearview mirror – Rückspiegel; **in the figurative sense** – im übertragenen Sinne; **septic tanks** – Jauchegruben, Klärtanks; **to swerve** – ausweichen

"Nonsense!" Justus took a deep breath. "Now think hard! After all, you are detectives!"
"Oh yeah? And who was the person that wasn't able to solve the puzzle for days himself? Wasn't that our First Detective in person?"
"But now I know what Tom referred to," Justus was sure. "And I tell you: it's totally simple! Just about every detective story reader might have come up with the answer by now, only we haven't!"
Peter shot through a side street. "Just, do you know how terrible you are when you are trying to give us clues? You should become a math teacher, not a detective!"
"Start with line two," Justus answered and repeated it: "*Every fug is known to him, there's nothing he can't disclose.*"
"Someone who is sticking his nose in everything," Bob interpreted the line.
"Exactly! Continue!", Justus said. "*In every country he exists and can easily be found!*"
"A snooper," Peter said. And suddenly he added in excitement: "A detective! They are everywhere!"
"**Score**! Of course a detective! When Sharky called us snoopers a little while ago it suddenly dawned on me. Stop, you have to turn left here!"
Just in time Peter could step on the brake. He had almost missed the street leading down to the harbor.
"*But if you want to find HIM, reach beyond your bounds!*"
"He refers to you, Justus!" Bob remarked. "Or rather to us. We are detectives. So we are supposed to reach beyond our own bounds if we want to find him."

---

score! – Treffer!

"Our area is Rocky Beach," Justus said. "If we reach beyond our bounds in the right spot, we're getting to …?"
"… Santa Monica!", Peter completed the sentence. He had arrived at the **intersection** with the street leading down to the harbor.
Justus pointed at a parking spot. "Park the car next to the police car. From here we have to walk."
In the meantime, Cotta was close behind them. Flashing his headlights at Peter, he passed him by and stopped in front of the police car. He got out, talked to the policeman, and pointed at Sharky sitting in the back seat of the car. The policeman nodded.
Peter turned off the car.
Cotta came up to them with fast steps. "I have asked another colleague to join me for support. And now, you detectives?"
"Now we are looking for *HIM*," Justus answered. "The detective Tom refers to in his puzzle. The one running the detective agency in Santa Monica."
"Dick Perry," Bob said.

---

intersection – Kreuzung

A False Game

"And where do we find Mr. Perry?", Cotta asked.
"We have to look for his boat. Its name is *Barbara.*"
"The name of his assistant," Cotta remembered.
"Come with us, Peter!" Justus shouted.
"But my clothes ..."
"Who cares! The T-Shirt is long enough!"
They started running into the direction of the pier.
Justus tried to spot what ships were anchoring where. There were more than enough boats here, and most of them were larger and more expensive than the one he was looking for. Finally, he discovered the boat in between several other small motorboats. Dick Perry was just about to **cast off**.
"Hurry up!" Justus shouted and squeezed himself through a small group of tourists standing in the way on the **landing stage**.
Peter was hardly able to follow him in his flip-flops; Bob and inspector Cotta were not very much faster.
Dick Perry heard Justus coming and stood up. He still held the **aft rope** in his hand.
Out of breath, Justus stood in front of him.
"What's up, fatty?" Perry was asking, **squinting** his eyes while looking at him. "Did you come here to congratulate me?"
Bob, Peter, and the inspector arrived. Perry took a step back.
"The case isn't fully solved yet," Justus explained. "Where is Betty Sutton?"

---

to cast off – ablegen, die Leinen losmachen; **landing stage** – Bootssteg; **aft rope** – Heckleine; **to squint** – blinzeln

"At the police station, of course!"
Justus shook his head and was just about to explain when suddenly the cabin door opened. Betty's head showed up. "Dick, what takes you so long to ...?"
She discovered the three detectives and stopped talking at once.
"Hello Barbara," Justus said soberly.
Puzzled, Peter and Bob looked at their friend.
"Barbara?"
"Barbara Stevens. Alias Betty Sutton," Justus introduced her. "Dick Perry's assistant. Meanwhile she's his **mistress**. Kidnapping and blackmail, Inspector. You can arrest them both."
"Ahem, yes, you are arrested, of course," Cotta mumbled, but his face was one big single question mark.
Dick Perry looked as if he had been hit by a baseball bat. His **superior** grin had completely disappeared from his face.
"*You* explain the whole story to the Inspector," he replied with a feeble voice.
Now it was Justus's turn to enjoy his triumph. "Dick Perry and Barbara Stevens! I assume you had been honest detectives in the past. Yes, that's how it must have started. You kept **suspects** under surveillance, solved cases, found out what illegal things other people were involved in. But one day things changed. You were **tempted** to **benefit** from other people's mistakes yourselves, instead of turning them over to the police. I don't know whether Sharky is the first case in this regard; at least, they found out that he had some **skeletons in the closet**. They took

---

mistress – Geliebte; **superior** – überlegen; **suspects** – Verdächtige; **to tempt** – verleiten, reizen; **to benefit** – einen Nutzen ziehen; **to have skeletons in the closet** – Dreck am Stecken, Leichen im Keller haben

photos of him, showing him how he entered his boat with stolen goods to bring them offshore. Using the false name 'Betty Sutton', Barbara sneaked into his house and started **spying** on him. The boat sank, and together they blackmailed him. We had come that far already." He looked around without saying anything else.

Peter and Bob nodded.

"Betty discovered the mail from Meg Baker, addressed to Sharky, and the whole plan was in danger. Mrs. Baker had to be kept away from the sunken boat. So you started the jellyfish action. One thing followed the other, and finally Meg Baker herself became part of the plan, as a victim. In that case the inheritance would have been the object of **desire**."

"You must still prove that," Dick Perry replied feebly.

"To keep everything under control Dick Perry wanted Mrs. Baker to hire him as a detective. Nothing easier than that: he simply dropped one of his flyers promoting his services in her mailbox. And Mrs. Baker took the **bait**. A nice double game! In this way, you would've had everything under perfect control. If it weren't for ... us also showing up at Mrs. Baker's place!"

"Indeed, you didn't really do me a favor with that," Perry mumbled.

"You succeeded in getting Mrs. Baker to make up her mind for you instead of us, but I managed to pass on the jellyfish e-mail on her computer to Tom Wood – and from here on, things went downhill for you. When you found out that he had been logging in to your computer you had to do something about him. With taking over the investigations you had everything

---

to spy (on so.) – (jmd. aus)spionieren; **desire** – Verlangen;
bait – Köder

under perfect control." Justus paused for a second and thought it over. Nearly everything was fitting together perfectly. "What I don't quite understand is why you destroyed our hard disk with that killer virus."

"I was afraid that you might have gotten a mail from Tom Wood, after all. And besides, I wanted to **obstruct** your investigations … and scare you a little, too ..."

Justus nodded. "We were a thorn in your flesh. But overall you had us under control at any time."

"It wasn't always that easy," Perry mumbled. His eyes had lost all traces of **slyness**.

Justus almost felt a little sympathetic for Dick Perry. "Well, I would have never guessed that we would win our detectivistic race now in this way. But **hats off** to you, Mr. Perry: the way you pretended **to expose** Betty Sutton was brilliant. We really bought it. It was both the most elegant and the cleverest way to escape. I assume you would have disappeared with the gold, never to show up again, right?"

"Right, because he had already closed down his office," Inspector Cotta suddenly added. "I found this out by pure coincidence from a colleague."

In the meantime Betty had gotten off the boat and stood next to Dick Perry. "We could have kept this on for years," she explained **sullenly**. "But we had to disappear because of you guys."

"Mr. Perry, after all you have saved my life," Peter remembered. "Down at the wreck. Why did you do that?"

Perry smiled. "I could answer now, I didn't want the boat to at-

---

to obstruct – behindern, blockieren; **slyness** – Listigkeit;
hats off – Hut ab; **to expose** – entlarven; **sullenly** – trotzig, mürrisch

tract even more attention than it already had. We wanted to use it as a base for the money handover. But that alone isn't it. Dead bodies are not part of our business. Barbara and me, we might work with tricks, but we would never put anyone's life at risk."
"Then Tom is still alive?"
"Of course." Perry pointed towards the boat. "He's in there. We would have set him free anyway."
"And you don't mention this until now!?" Justus left the group standing there and jumped aboard. With a quick grip he opened the cabin door and stepped down inside. "Tom! Are you here? Tom!"
Somewhere he heard some faint knocking. Justus turned around. It came from a **chest** in the back.
Justus walked up to it, opened the **latch**, and lifted the **lid**.
The familiar face of Tom Wood appeared. It was a little **wrinkled-up**, but now he was smiling. "Hi, Just! That was about time! Does it always take you so long to solve a puzzle?"
Justus hesitated for a moment. Then, with a broad grin, he answered:
"If you suddenly discover a major crime –
you had better speak up clearly in time!"

---

chest (hier) – Kiste, Truhe; **latch** – Riegel, Verschluss;
lid – Deckel; **wrinkled-up** – zerknittert